DOCTOR DIANA

DOCTOR DIANA

Jessica Blake

CHIVERS
THORNDIKE

This Large Print book is published by BBC Audiobooks Ltd, Bath, England and by Thorndike Press®, Waterville, Maine, USA.

Published in 2005 in the U.K. by arrangement with the Author.

Published in 2005 in the U.S. by arrangement with Juliet Burton Literary Agency.

U.K. Hardcover ISBN 1–4056–3425–1 (Chivers Large Print)
U.S. Softcover ISBN 0–7862–7803–X (Buckinghams)

The text of this Large Print edition is unabridged.
Other aspects of the book may vary from the original edition.

Set in 16 pt. New Times Roman.

Printed in Great Britain on acid-free paper.

British Library Cataloguing in Publication Data available

Library of Congress Cataloging-in-Publication Data

Blake, Jessica.
    Doctor Diana / by Jessica Blake.
       p.   cm.
    "Thorndike Press large print Buckinghams"—T.p. verso.
    ISBN 0–7862–7803–X (lg. print : sc : alk. paper)
    1. Women physicians—Fiction. 2. Hong Kong (China)—Fiction.
    3. Large type books. I. Title.
PS3602.L345D63 2005
813'.6—dc22   2005011960

CHAPTER ONE

The jumbo zoomed down to Kai Tak airport, skimming the harbour like a gigantic seagull landing upon a reef. As the aircraft touched down on the single runway surrounded by water, and the island of Hong Kong rose majestically to its peak on one side, with Kowloon opposite set against a backdrop of mountains, Diana gasped and the white-haired man sitting next to her smiled.

'Didn't you know that Hong Kong's airstrip sliced across the middle of the harbour?' he asked.

She shook her head. 'I took it for granted that it would be on dry land, like other airports.'

'Well, in a way it is. Like Kowloon itself, it is built on land reclaimed from the sea, but because of the limitations of the harbour area there can only be one runway and therefore only one aircraft can take off or land at a time. Touching down is a bit hair-raising the first time you experience it, but I've never heard of an accident since the airport was built.'

Pearl Wong might have warned me, all the same, Diana thought as her heartbeats steadied. After all, Pearl was Hong Kong born and bred, and an air-stewardess with Ta'i Airways into the bargain—but for those very reasons she probably just took it all for granted.

Pearl, her flat-mate in London until the day before yesterday, had all the seemingly helpless charm of the oriental female and could consequently be forgiven much. Especially since she had been instrumental in putting as great a distance as possible between Diana and the remnants of a broken love affair. To have continued to live in the flat below Clive would have been intolerable. Even to remain in the same city would have been intolerable. Several thousand miles were a good safeguard against bumping into him in the street, but promised to be little safeguard against memory. He had scarcely been out of her mind during the flight from London. Even the current movie had turned the knife in the wound, being a story about a talented scenic designer who might have been based on Clive himself—handsome, and devilishly attractive.

Her elderly neighbour studied her now, as he had secretly studied her all the way, without appearing to. Being nearly seventy, he felt he could safely display an interest in a pretty girl without that interest being misconstrued. Right from the take-off he had been aware of an inner tension about her, and his experienced eye had noticed a hidden sadness in her face. She had also avoided conversation, spending most of her waking hours reading or listening to music, and after briefly watching a

2

film which he would have expected any young and modern girl to find distinctly appealing, since it was high comedy that dealt with a young and modern man, she had closed her eyes, taken the ear-phones out of her ears to cut off the sound track, and not glanced at the screen again. And at Bahrain and Bangkok, when passengers were allowed to stretch their legs in the airport transit lounge, she had kept herself strictly to herself; not actually rebuffing any conversational overtures, but not encouraging them, either.

Such reserve in one so young seemed, to his professional mind, to be unnatural. It went deeper than shyness, as if she had withdrawn into herself, but now, as the whole glittering panorama of Hong Kong harbour opened up, she too seemed to expand. Gazing through the aircraft window, her eyes were touched with sudden anticipation.

He ventured to ask, 'Is this your first visit to Hong Kong?'

She nodded.

'And how long are you staying?'

'Two years minimum.' She added, 'That's my official duty tour.'

A layman would have asked what she meant by that, but he merely remarked, 'So you're in medicine.'

Again she nodded. 'Newly qualified, I admit.'

'I would have guessed so, judging by your

youth.'

For the first time, she really looked at him. Throughout the flight she had paid little attention to the kindly old gentleman sitting beside her, but now, as the aircraft trundled to a halt and she unfastened her seat belt and twenty-odd hours of travelling came to an end, she felt a little guilty for having taken so little notice of him. His eyes were kind, and the curiosity he displayed was nothing but fatherly.

'If you have signed on for a two-year duty tour,' he said, 'that means you've taken a house job in a hospital.' His eyes twinkled. 'I know something about the medical profession, my dear. I was in it for many years. May I ask which hospital you are going to?'

'The Kinsale.'

Diana thought she detected a certain surprise and pleasure in his face, but there was no time for further conversation. The flight was over. People were gathering up hand luggage. The old gentleman took down her coat from the locker above, and handed it to her.

'I trust you are being met?'

'Thank you, yes. I was told that transport would be sent for me.'

'Then I'll say goodbye and good luck. No doubt I shall have the pleasure of meeting you again. Sooner or later everybody meets everybody in this colony.'

He gave a courtly little bow and departed.

She was almost sorry to see him go. Plunging into the whirl of Kai Tak airport was a bewildering experience to someone who had never set foot in the East. The babel of voices and multi-racial languages almost deafened her, but somehow she battled her way through the formalities, and then emerged on to a startling scene.

Rows of young Chinese men stood in line beyond the exit, holding placards aloft advertising hotels or displaying the names of passengers for whom they waited. Shouts and ringing bells mingled with sing-song chatter and high-pitched laughter. Names were also being shouted through loudspeakers.

'Meester and Meeses Kellee, plees! Meester and Meeses Kellee! You are awaited in the first class arrival lounge . . .' 'Colonel Par-ker, plees! Colonel Par-ker, plees—your car awaits in car park. Plees to call at Desk Fife for kees!'

And then Diana's own name, coming as something of a shock as she stood there, not knowing where to go next and fumbling in her purse for what she hoped would be the right amount of Hong Kong currency to pay the Chinese porter, who had already dumped her bags and was waiting with oriental passivity.

'Dok-tor Free-man, plees! Dok-tor Di-anna Free-man, plees! Plees to go to Desk Seex— Desk Seex, plees!'

The porter had gone. She could grapple with one bag plus hand luggage, but not three.

And where in heaven's name was desk six? Behind her in the reception hall, of course. A porter—another porter! Or leave her bags out here and hope to find them again in this whirling throng?

Since every porter in sight was occupied, she had no choice. She grabbed the lightest bag because it was the most valuable and contained her stethoscope. How proud she had been when she had bought it, and how proud Clive had been, too, in his amused sort of way. He had come along with her to John Bell & Croyden in Wigmore Street, and stood there with that quizzical smile on his face while she examined a selection. Why couldn't he take her as seriously as the man behind the counter, she had thought, feeling self-conscious only because Clive looked on with such indulgent amusement. And when the shop assistant placed the treasured instrument in a box and carefully wrapped it, and then packaged the other essential medical equipment she had bought, Clive had murmured for her ear alone, 'Sorry, my darling, but I just can't think of you as a fully fledged doctor. You're too pretty to have a brain in your head!'

'Would you like to see my M.B. diploma? Or better still my ratings? My marks were high, let me tell you!'

'I give you high marks myself, sweet, but for other things than brains . . .'

6

Why did she have to remember that conversation now, as she battled her way through jostling shoulders across the Kai Tak's central hall? She had come to Hong Kong to forget Clive, to make a new start, find a new life, not to drag memories of the old one with her, and particularly not *his* memory. But even against this unfamiliar scene his face seemed to stand out in her mind. How long would it take to forget his bearded features, not to mention his passion and his tenderness and his ability to stir her blood?

She stumbled to a halt, aware that tears were dangerously close. Homesickness, of course—that was all it was. And tiredness too. She recognized the symptoms of fatigue. The trouble was that when it came to herself she was no more able to combat them than any other young woman, particularly a young woman whose heart had been hurt.

Her name was being called again. 'Dok-tor Free-man, plees to go to Desk Seex!'

And there it was, ahead of her, and leaning against the counter, looking both bored and impatient, was a tall young man wearing blue denims and Hawaiian shirt, with a shock of blond hair and a sulky touch to his mouth which told her all too plainly that he had been waiting for a long time and didn't like it. He was there on compulsion, no more. For a cab driver, this struck her as insolent, so she made her voice especially cool as she announced to the Chinese desk clerk, 'My name has been called. I am Doctor Freeman.'

The blond young man jerked to attention, surveyed her for one astonished moment, then said in a decidedly English voice, 'Good grief, you can't be!'

He was no cab driver, with a voice like that, an accent like that. A member of the hospital administrative staff, perhaps. A clerk or an assistant in the hospital secretary's office, delegated to meet the newest addition to the medical staff, and possessing the typical attitude of Admin. to medicos.

'And why can't I be?' she retorted, the coolness still in her voice.

The young man ran a hand through his thick hair, laughing uneasily. 'Well, dammit, the way you look! The last woman doctor we had was as round as the Albert Hall, with legs that would have supported a grand piano and a voice like a sergeant major!'

'But no doubt a very good doctor.'

He didn't miss the ice in her voice, and got the message. *Just because I'm a doctor doesn't mean I'm not feminine, and just because I'm feminine doesn't mean I can't be a doctor, and a good one too.*

He could almost see the defensive sparks flying, which meant, of course, that she had already come up against the scepticism with which some people, even today, viewed young women doctors. He was sorry at once, and

8

said so.

'Look—let's start off on the right foot, shall we? I'm Chris Muldoon, your counterpart in Surgery. Like you, I'm in my first house job.' He held out his hand, grinning, and she was glad to take it. It was good to have a friendly hand to grasp. Her own smile flashed in return, and he looked at her with even greater approval. 'You should do that more often, Doc. It melts the ice in your face. Let's be on our way, shall we? Where are your bags?'

'Outside, on the pavement. I had to leave them—'

'Good grief! Then say a prayer and make a dash for it before they're snatched—if they haven't been already!'

He propelled her forcefully back to the exit, telling her cheerfully not to worry if they had vanished because whatever was lost could easily be replaced. 'There's nowhere in the world like Hong Kong for shopping, particularly clothes. You can get all you want, as fabulous as you want, for whatever price you want, and as quickly as you want.'

'Providing one has the money, Mr. Muldoon, which a newly qualified house physician in her first job won't have until her first pay cheque comes along. And don't look at me as if I were an idiot for abandoning my bags. What else could I do? I'm not a female coolie.'

He laughed. '*I'll* say. But remember you're

9

in Hong Kong, the vice den of the world—or so the rest of the world says. And not without cause, though the old opium smuggling days are over, except for peddlers with their little white packets. Don't look so startled, Dr. Freeman—the Hong Kong police are the finest in the world, and you can always count on my good straight right for protection.'

They were outside again, facing the barricade of Chinese boys with their advertising placards—and there, to Diana's relief, were her bags, safe and sound, with a couple of small Chinese children sitting on them, looking like oriental dolls.

'Ha!' exclaimed Chris Muldoon. 'Young Charlie and Kathy Yengtoh, plying their trade again.' He fished in his pocket for coins and thrust them into small outstretched hands. The doll-like faces beamed, tilted eyes twinkled, small bodies bowed low and then raced off, eagerly searching for more luggage to guard. 'They do a roaring trade, those kids. The Hong Kong Chinese are gluttons for work, in other words money, from an early age.'

Diana took her small case while Chris Muldoon carried the other two.

'You mean those tiny tots spend their time down here at the airport, keeping an eye on people's luggage?'

'It's better than begging. This way for the car park —'

Using her bags to push a track through the

crowd, the young house surgeon continued, 'You'll soon grow accustomed to the Hong Kong Chinese capacity for work. The parents of those kids start at six in the morning and go on till midnight, six days a week. The seventh, Sunday, is a holiday—they finish at noon.' He laughed at her horror-struck face. 'You'll come across the Yengtohs. They run one of the best dressmaking establishments on Kowloon side, and I'll bet my bottom Hong Kong dollar that you'll have at least one gown made by Mrs. Yengtoh and her daughters—for the Kinsale Hospital Ball perhaps—because any woman who wants to be really beautifully dressed can't afford *not* to go to Yengtoh's Salon on Mody Road, just as every well-dressed man in the colony makes sure of having his suits made by Mr. Yengtoh and his sons. And there isn't a person working in the establishment who doesn't bear the family name. As soon as young Charlie and Kathy leave school—oh yes, they do go to school, in between plying their trade at the airport—they'll be trained by Mum and Dad and their elder sisters and brothers, all of whom have Western Christian names. That's the custom in Hong Kong. Charles and James and Stuart, Elizabeth and Margaret and Anne are particular favourites, being associated with Royalty. Here we are— and I hope you're suitably impressed by your transport, Doctor. Hell, I can't go on calling you that! Diana, isn't it?'

She nodded, scarcely attending. She had expected nothing so splendid as a Jaguar to meet her. A hospital bus, perhaps, or a taxi, but nothing so grand as this.

Chris Muldoon, stowing her bags in the capacious boot, grinned again. 'Not mine, needless to say. Wish it were. You would have been insulted if I'd brought my broken-down jalopy. This splendid affair belongs to the Super, no less.'

'The medical superintendent—sending his own car!'

Chris handed her inside, then slid into the driving seat.

'Not exactly. Jonathan Kinsale is the last man to lay on anything special for a woman member of the staff, other than Matron, of course. Matrons always have to be kowtowed to, as you probably know. But someone had to meet you, and there wasn't a hospital car available, nor any other member of the staff but me. I thought that was my misfortune until I saw you. In the ordinary way I hate hanging about airports, waiting for delayed aircraft, and yours was nearly a couple of hours late.'

'I could see your frustration,' she answered wryly, 'but perhaps the chance to drive such a car as this made up for it? And how did I come to be so honoured?'

'It was Matron's doing, really. No other vehicle was free, and in any case, apart from ambulances the hospital has only a couple of staff cars to its name and both were needed for running home a couple of discharged patients. You'll get used to that sort of informal service; the Kinsale is still very much a small family hospital. Matron herself doesn't run a car because she swears that driving in the streets of Kowloon is playing with death—' He swerved violently to avoid a racing cab and then again, even more violently, to dodge a couple of jog-trotting rickshaws hidden behind. Matron, thought Diana, seemed to have a point.

'So there was only the Super's car or mine,' Chris Muldoon rattled on, 'and mine broke down on the road to Repulse Bay this morning and had to be towed away. But Kinsale's Jag was standing out in the courtyard doing nothing. Matron pointed to it so significantly that he could scarcely refuse, especially when she scotched his idea of sending a taxi to pick you up. She called that a cold sort of welcome for someone arriving at Kai Tak for the first time. She's all for the personal touch, is Matron. Not so Jonathan Kinsale! If it had been left to him, you could have walked and carried your bags the whole way.'

'The man's a monster!'

'Not really. He's just indifferent to women. Don't get me wrong—I don't mean that way. Once upon a time he was very partial to the opposite sex, or so I've heard, but something happened to turn him off. What, I don't know, though there have been all sorts of rumours, all adding up to the same thing—that somewhere along the line he was crossed in love, to use an old-fashioned phrase, and turned his back on the whole scene from then on.'

By now he had nosed the car out of the airport and towards Kowloon City, still talking. 'I don't know how genned up you are on the history of the Kinsale Hospital, but it was founded by a Dr. Joseph Kinsale in 1874, and every succeeding generation of the family has served it. That's why we have a Kinsale as our current superintendent, even though he's a surgeon and, as you know, the medical superintendent of a hospital is usually a physician. However, the Kinsale runs independently in its own way—and so does Jonathan Kinsale. Be armed against him, fair Diana.'

'Why? Is he an ogre, or something?'

'The staff sometimes thinks so, though really we all admire his dedication, not only to the hospital, but to his work. It is life itself to him. Snag is, he thinks it should be the same to everyone else. Don't let him work you too hard.'

But that was what she wanted, total occupation. Total oblivion in mind-absorbing work. No job could be too arduous, no hours too long to fill the aching void in her heart, the void which Clive had left. Not that he had done so deliberately. He hadn't jilted her for

14

anyone else—not anyone specific, at least. There had merely been a lessening of his ardour; fewer phone calls, fewer rings of the front door bell, fewer halts on his way upstairs to his flat, even when he knew Pearl was away on a flight and that consequently they would have the place to themselves; fewer dates and fewer attempts to arrange them; a lack of enthusiasm in his voice when she telephoned him; evasions and excuses. All the frightening symptoms of the slow death of an affair, even though he still said that he loved her.

'A fire may die down a bit, honey, that's all. But remember, it can always flare up again.'

'Or die completely,' she had answered. 'I don't think I want to stay around to find out.'

He had shrugged at that. 'The choice is yours. We're both free, so neither of us can gripe if the other wants to take off. I'm not making any claims.'

Why had she felt that somehow he had made her say the very thing he wanted to hear, do the very thing he wanted her to do? Clive had always had the uncanny knack of making others reach decisions they had not really been contemplating. Hers had been to end their affair before the embers were totally dead. That way, at least, a small glow remained, and she saved a few fragments of her pride as well.

And Pearl had helped her. In retrospect, it seemed as if Pearl had jumped at the chance.

'My brother runs the family law firm in

Hong Kong and handles all the legal affairs of the Kinsale Hospital. I know the place has difficulty in getting staff because the two major hospitals, the Queen Elizabeth on Kowloon side and the Queen Mary on Hong Kong side, are bigger and richer and pay higher salaries. But a newly qualified doctor could get good experience at the Kinsale. Shall I write to Lee and tell him about you? If any vacancy is likely, he can find out.'

Why not? She had nothing to lose. And probably nothing to gain either, because vacancies didn't just occur at conveniently opportune moments. So she let Pearl go ahead, and meanwhile applied for house jobs at British provincial hospitals and avoiding the London ones, because her need to get away from all reminder of Clive was so great, but the most she had achieved were promises 'in the event of a house vacancy occurring', which left Diana still occupying the flat below his and listening for his footsteps overhead or on the stairs, straining her ears every time he had company, trying to identify the feminine voice or the feminine laughter and wishing to heaven she could get as far away as possible.

She had reached the stage of answering ads in the medical journals for temporary locums, when the miracle happened. The Kinsale Hospital in Hong Kong needed a junior house physician, the salary minimal, interviews to take place in London, and the successful

16

applicant's flight paid when taking up the appointment and at the end of it, but not for leaves in between. Niggardly terms, by U.K. and other standards, 'But beginners can't be choosers,' she commented cheerfully to Pearl as she headed for the telephone and called the medical agency conducting the interviews.

Her heart sank when she learned that she would have to wait four days, the list of applicants already being long. It seemed that every newly qualified Bachelor of Medicine in London was eager to go abroad. By the time she arrived for the first interview she was convinced that some prior applicant had already beaten her to it, and was therefore surprised when she was summoned for a second and then a third and final one, and even more unbelieving when she received an official letter offering her the job. Within a week, she was on her way.

Pearl was delighted, though she declared that she hated Diana's going. 'Goodness knows how I shall find a flatmate as nice as you, but we'll see each other every time I fly in to Kai Tak, and my family will make you welcome. They live on the Mid-Levels—that's half way up the Peak—and know absolutely everybody, both Western and Chinese. It is a very integrated society there.'

The airport was left behind and Chris Muldoon's voice was saying, 'That's the Sung Wong Toi monument we're passing right now.

It commemorates the Emperor of the Sung Dynasty who took refuge in Kowloon. The Cantonese name for Kowloon is Tsim Sha Tsui, but now it only applies to the main business centre.'

He turned right at traffic lights, still talking. 'That's the Peninsula Hotel on the left hand corner, commonly known as The Royal Household because there isn't a crowned head in Europe which hasn't stayed there. It's one of the most famous hotels in the world and Gaddi's, its leading restaurant, is listed amongst the world's Top Seven. The Peninsula Lobby is famous as a meeting place for East and West, and something not to be missed. Now we're in Nathan Road. Would you believe that only sixty-odd years ago there wasn't a building in sight? Nothing but an unmade country road lined with trees. And now look at it!'

Diana was looking. Vivid Chinese shop signs and banners not only adorned the buildings and projected over the pavements, but were festooned across the street like gigantic Christmas decorations. Jewellers and boutiques, night clubs and discos; fashion stores selling the latest creations from Paris and London and New York; windows filled with ivory, jade, exotic flowers, precious metals, aromatic herbs and foodstuffs; topless bars next door to temples, Lutheran chapels cheek by jowl with strip clubs; cinemas showing porn films alongside sedate antique dealers and prestige stores, and nobody taking any notice of anybody; women walking unmolested in the streets, tea salons packed with Chinese families playing Mahjong at crowded tables, and everything seemingly calm and serene beneath the teaming life.

'It's fantastic!' Diana breathed.

'The whole story of Hong Kong is fantastic. I'll tell it to you sometime, but not now—we're nearly at the hospital.'

The Jag whipped round a corner, narrowly missing a small Chinese boy carrying a long pole stacked with a multitude of Chinese lanterns, and another bearing a laden tray on his head from which an appetizing smell steamed from beneath a hot damp cloth. On the right were trees.

'This is Haiphong Road, and on the right is Kowloon Park. The hospital overlooks it at one side. One thing in favour of the Kinsale is its situation—we're not hemmed in by buildings as we would be in Mongkok or Wanchai, thanks to the Kinsale family acquiring the site back in the eighteen-hundreds and fighting to have the adjoining area preserved as a park and recreation ground. If you're lucky, you may even have a room overlooking it.'

The Jaguar zoomed to a halt. They were in a courtyard fronting a sedate Victorian building with a flight of stone steps leading up to the entrance.

'Well, here we are,' Chris Muldoon announced cheerfully. 'Now you have to face the monster—and good luck to you.'

CHAPTER TWO

Jonathan Kinsale finished operating shortly after six. In the scrubbing-up room Staff Nurse Chang, from Lotus Ward, removed his surgical apron, untied his mask, peeled off his skin-rubber gloves, and departed with the spoils to the chute which went straight down to the cleansing room. Jonathan stepped out of his rubber boots, pulled off his surgical cap, and began to scrub his sinewy arms and hands.

'A good afternoon's work,' he said to his assistant. 'A diverticulum can be a tricky thing, but that man will live, thank God.'

Thanks weren't entirely due to God, thought Maynard, the resident surgical officer, except for endowing Jonathan Kinsale with so much skill and intelligence.

'A very good afternoon's work,' the man agreed, 'but you need a rest, if I may say so. You're working as hard as any member of the medical staff, even though you are now superintendent with all the extra work that goes with it. Most Supers ease off when those additional responsibilities are thrust on them.'

20

'Well, don't expect *me* to. I'd be bored.'

There were ways of alleviating boredom, the other man thought. Especially in Hong Kong. But it was characteristic of Jonathan Kinsale not to think of that.

'At least pressure should relax a bit now the new house physician has come,' Maynard said. 'That releases Muldoon from the extra medical duties he's taken on, and leaves him free for surgery—which is what he's here for.'

'The new house physician has to prove himself yet.'

'*Him*self; sir? I heard it was a woman.'

'I forgot.' Jonathan Kinsale threw aside his towel, rolled down his shirt sleeves, opened his locker and pulled on his jacket. 'Yes, the new house physician *is* a woman, more's the pity. We seem to get very little choice these days, what with America and other countries enticing British doctors away and we, alas, being unable to compete financially with the Government-run hospitals here. So I suppose we must just make the best of a bad job.'

'Why should it be bad, sir? There are many out-standing women doctors.'

'Outstanding because they are in the minority, and are therefore noticed more.'

'You don't approve of women in medicine?' enquired Maynard.

'On the nursing side, yes. There, they are admirable. A pity they don't remain there. The trouble today is that women won't stay in their

21

rightful places. All this women's lib stuff makes them want to invade ours.' He flashed his rare and unexpected smile. 'But take no notice of me. My father says I'm bigoted.'

And your father could be right, thought the R.S.O.

The door from the operating theatre swung on silent hinges, revealing Staff Nurse Chang again—petite, dark and pretty. Rumour had it she was in love with Chris Muldoon, but hospitals were full of rumours and Muldoon's life was full of pretty girls.

'The hospital secretary on the phone, Mr. Kinsale. He asked me to tell you that Dr. Freeman has arrived and is waiting in your office.'

'Good. Have some tea sent along for her, will you? I expect someone arriving from England would be glad of it. And let her know I'll be along shortly. I have to visit the registrar first.'

He left the theatre, walking with his long easy stride. At the hissing sterilizer a young theatre nurse watched him depart, and sighed inwardly. He was so aloof, so reserved, and so distinguished with that premature silver at the temples. And that reserve of his was positively challenging, she thought romantically.

Sister Theatre thought the same thing, but in a more restrained fashion. Sister Theatre was Helen Collard in off-duty hours, but the Kinsale Hospital still clung to the old-fashioned way of calling Sisters by the names of their departments or wards, and would never dream of using the term 'nursing officer'. Hence Sister Theatre, Sister X-Rays, Sister Casualty. Ward Sisters fared better, because the wards at Kinsale were called after flowers. Sister Theatre would very much have preferred to be known as Sister Lotus, Sister Magnolia, Sister Cherry-blossom or Sister Freesia. Nothing could be more unromantic than being associated with an operating theatre, she thought wryly as she stepped out of the way to let Davis, the cockney theatre orderly, hose down the tiled walls.

'Well,' the man threw over his shoulder, 'the Lord'n Master did a good job this afternoon, didn't he? Gotta hand it to him, Great Mogul though he is.'

Sister Theatre smiled and went into the anteroom to bring the day's records up-to-date. There was a lot in what Davis said. Apart from the diverticulum today, he had done a laporotomy which revealed worse trouble than anticipated, but the patient would live. Jonathan Kinsale was certainly a fine surgeon, but it was a pity the man was so unapproachable. Many of the staff thought him inhuman because he didn't unbend occasionally, but Matron had once confided that in her opinion that was due to a reserve which amounted almost to shyness; as for Sister Theatre herself; she knew that a man so devoted to saving human life couldn't be a mere machine. Somewhere beneath that cold exterior lay a heart, even if only for physiological reasons.

Behind her, Staff Nurse Chang picked up the house phone, got through to the kitchen and ordered tea to be sent along to the Super's office.

Was it for the Super himself? No. In that case, the kitchen grumbled, it would have to wait. The kitchen was busy. The kitchen was short-staffed, and didn't she realise that? Dorothy Chang, whose English mother had been a nurse and whose Chinese father was a doctor, sighed good-naturedly.

'All right, I can take a hint. I'm free for half an hour anyway,' and down she went to collect the tea herself. The thought of any nurse demeaning herself in such a way in the English hospital where she had been sent for training, made her smile. But this was the Kinsale in Hong Kong, where everyone had to pull together. At least it made for a less formal atmosphere. As Matron loved to say, 'We're one big happy family here!' but that was usually when she wanted someone to do an extra chore or two. In this instance, Dorothy Chang didn't mind. She wanted to see what the new house-phiz was like, anyway.

To say that she was surprised by her first glimpse of Dr. Freeman was, as she confided in the Nurses' Home later, putting it more than mildly. It wasn't so much that she was surprised by her youth—newly qualified doctors were usually young, unless they had studied late in life—as by her looks, which really did load the dice against the nurses who had to wear the Kinsale's unbecoming uniform. No ugly little starched cap would adorn young Dr. Freeman's flaming Titian hair, which could be displayed without restriction and not even Matron could object.

It was rather hard, being a nurse under a Matron who clung to old-fashioned ideas, such as no make-up when on duty and hair screwed back into a neat bun if it happened to be long. But in other ways Matron wasn't a bad old girl, thought Staff Nurse Chang philosophically, so one had to count one's blessings.

Diana Freeman was standing by the window, looking down on to Kowloon Park, when the door opened. Against her will, she was thinking of home—which meant Clive of course. Somehow the whole landscape outside this window made her homesick for everything she had left behind, so the sight of a nurse entering with tea made her almost want to cry.

'How kind of you!' she exclaimed as the girl set down the tray.

'It wasn't my idea, Doctor. It was Mr. Kinsale's.'

'The Super? But I understood he was a monster!'

'Who told you that?'

25

'The young man who met me at the airport. I gather the medical superintendent is a slave-driver, and somehow I don't associate kindly thoughts with that type.'

'She knew she was speaking unwisely. Nerves, of course. She would have to be more discreet, because Nurses' Homes were notorious for hospital gossip and no doubt every word of this conversation would be reported over supper there this evening.

And now this attractive girl, a fascinating combination of oriental and western blood, seemed to be lingering for a chat.

'Mr. Kinsale asked me to tell you that he'll be along soon. He had to visit the registrar first. I'm Chang, from Lotus Ward. That's on Surgical, so I was allowed to do theatre duty this afternoon—the patient was one of mine. A diverticulum. He did a wonderful job—Mr. Kinsale, I mean. But he always does. And I shouldn't take too much notice of what Chris Muldoon says. From the sound of things, it's he you've been talking to. He says a lot of things he doesn't really mean. Actually, he's Mr. Kinsale's most ardent admirer, though he would never admit it. One day he'll be a replica of Mr. Kinsale, though from the way he sometimes behaves many people wouldn't think so. But when you see Chris at work, you won't see a trace of that scattiness of his.'

She seemed anxious to defend the young man, which was significant. Diana smiled and said soothingly, 'I guessed he was good at his job, Staff Nurse.' She had noted the girl's rank from the belt she wore.

Dorothy tried to keep the envy out of her voice as she answered, 'So it *was* he who met you . . .'

'Yes.'

That's surprising, thought the nurse. Today's his off-duty and I felt sure he'd be spending it with that girl Estelle from Government House—all Roedean airs and graces. Or even one of those Escort girls, if he could afford one.

'Well, I'd better be on my way . . .'

She gave her friendly smile and departed, although she would have liked to find out more; just how Chris came to be meeting the new house-phiz, for instance, though that could well have been Matron's doing. Even medicos jumped to attention when her voice was heard. Even more important, how had Chris reacted to this gorgeous redhead? He had a weakness for a pretty face, as she, who had loved him since he first came to the Kinsale, very well knew. And, knowing him so well, she could imagine his appreciative eye taking in every detail of this girl's lissom figure.

Dorothy Chang, as petite as all oriental women, looked with envy on Diana's height which, although not above average for a western woman, seemed desirably tall to her.

Coupled with that, Diana's ability to wear clothes well was a further cause for envy. The slim lines of her body well displayed the white drill slacks and blazer which she had bought especially for the Hong Kong climate, and beneath the blazer she wore a sleeveless silk sweater in emerald green, the polo collar at her throat being a dramatic foil for her vivid colouring. Her eyes were large and deepset, and her skin that creamy colour which reminded little Nurse Chang of magnolia petals, delicately tinged with pink on the cheekbones.

As for her nose—Dorothy regarded that with particular envy, being herself possessed of the diminutive snub nose which adorned many an oriental face and which she therefore regarded as commonplace. Such a word could never be applied to young Dr. Freeman's short patrician nose, straight cut and delicate, nor to her oval chin, which somehow added sensitivity to her lovely face.

Walking along the corridor, little Nurse Chang caught sight of herself in the glass of a swing door and sighed. No one could call *me* pretty! Half and half, that's me. She didn't believe her loving parents when they truthfully told her she had inherited the best of both their looks, nor Chris when he said the same thing. 'That oriental touch makes you vastly intriguing, Lotus Blossom, but I guess you know that. I guess you've been told how fascinating you are, hundreds of times.'

He could natter on like that *ad infinitum*, and it didn't mean a thing.

*   *   *

Diana drank the tea gratefully. It was a nice gesture for a monster to make, she reflected, so perhaps the man wasn't so bad after all. Whatever she did, she must avoid listening to hospital gossip or personal opinions, a maxim she had learned at her teaching hospital, where gossip had been particularly rampant. Wherever there were medical students of both sexes there would always be name-linking and even scandal. One merely shrugged it off. But here it would be different. Her student days were over and she was facing the real thing; responsibility and work, diagnosis and treatment. There would be no one to tell her what to do or how to do it, and the nurses would blame her if her prescriptions and treatments failed. And not only the nurses. Sisters could be particularly snooty and Matrons positively scathing.

Hospital staffs were among the most critical in the world. She had seen newly-qualified doctors being watched and silently judged by senior doctors and surgeons, not to mention nurses and patients, all waiting for them to make a slip. Oh, dear God, she thought, I wish I were home! I'm frightened.

The door opened. Diana jerked round, splashing tea down the lapels of her white drill blazer. She stared in dismay, standing there before the medical superintendent. What a beginning! She whipped out a tissue and dabbed ineffectively.

'That won't be much use. Try this—'

But he didn't give her a chance to wield his large handkerchief; he was doing that himself already, and very competently. His hand was long and finely shaped; a surgeon's hand, with the delicate and sure touch of his profession.

'That's got the worst out, but I advise you to send it down to the hospital laundry. They have cleaning facilities there.'

He went round to the other side of his big desk and nodded to her to be seated in the armchair opposite. She saw a man with keen eyes, a mouth which might be humorous if ever permitted to be, and features symmetrical and well cut. The touch of silver at his temples gave him an air of distinction, but he would still be distinguished even without it, she thought.

She found herself studying him quite dispassionately and with considerable interest. His hair was black, throwing those silver streaks into dramatic contrast; his nose rather large, high-bridged, and proud—a clear-cut, aquiline nose which indicated strength of character. Before he sat down she noticed his unusual height, in comparison with which she felt small and very feminine. Further strength was indicated in the solid bulk of the man, the breadth of shoulder, the jutting angle of his chin—the cleft chin which so frequently characterised the dominant male. His eyes compelled attention; they were so deepset that it was hard to tell whether they were very dark grey or very deep hazel. Whatever their colour, they were riveting, giving the impression that they looked right into the depths of her mind and that to hide anything from them would be impossible.

There was a dynamic quality about this man which disturbed her. He was not to be lightly dismissed, or merely regarded as an aggressive boss. His looks were memorable, not merely because they were handsome but because they were striking; the kind of looks a woman noticed at first glance and recalled long after a man passed.

He wasn't a bit what she expected, though what she actually had expected she wasn't quite sure. A monster had to be stern and terrifying, or at the very least brisk and possibly caustic. This man was none of those things. He was quiet and courteous, but she guessed he would have no truck with pretence.

She was right. He came to the point at once.

'It is my duty to welcome you here, Doctor. The medical agency thought you were the most suitable candidate, and we accept their recommendation because its Appointments

Board of qualified medical specialists has always proved reliable—'

'—but you are not happy about it personally,' Diana heard herself interrupt, and bit her lip. The worst thing a junior could do was to interrupt a senior. This beginning was going from bad to worse. She apologised at once.

'No need—you are absolutely right,' he said. 'I do have a personal bias against women doctors, but I am in the minority, so you need pay no heed to that.'

'It will be hard not to, since you are superintendent here. Your aversion puts me under a handicap from the start.' Fatigue and disappointment made her reckless, and she didn't care when his eyebrows rose. She went on indignantly, 'You will be judging me in advance on everything I do. Condemning me, too!' Indignation made her voice shake.

'And not without reason, it seems. You are demonstrating the very thing I have against women doctors—their emotional instability. Women live on their emotions, but a good doctor cannot afford them. Nurses can become emotionally involved with their patients— indeed, it very often helps if they do, it makes them care about them more—but a medical practitioner must remain calm at all times and never allow emotion to upset judgment. You have done precisely that already. However, since you *are* here, let me say that I hope you will be happy and serve this hospital well. The Kinsale means a lot to me.'

'And work means a lot to me, sir.'

She had control of herself now. She wasn't going to allow this man to upset her further, and was certainly never going to let him see anything but her cool, efficient front. Only to herself had she ever admitted that a front would always be essential to her. She loved caring for patients, loved medicine as much as her father had done, but in the real live hospital world she wouldn't be tending her dolls, as she had done in childhood. She would be face to face with suffering humanity and responsible for it. As this man said, a doctor couldn't afford to have emotions, much less show them.

'Another reason for my aversion to women doctors,' he went on, 'is their regrettable tendency to marry. As soon as that happens, their work takes second place. A married woman with a career is nothing but a nuisance. She either sacrifices her family for her job, or her job for her family. Either way, she is unreliable.'

Bigotry! Sheer bigotry! Diana fought for self-control, and found it.

'Let me assure you, sir, that I shall most certainly not marry or prove unreliable. I came here to do a job and I shall do it.'

Unimpressed, he retorted, 'You will have to answer to me if you don't.' His steely eyes surveyed her and for a moment a flicker of amusement seemed to be there. Then he asked in an offhand way, 'What made you go in for medicine?'

'I always wanted to. My father wanted it too, but unlike you he didn't think me unsuitable or incapable.'

He ignored that and rose, dismissing her.

'You will report for duty in twenty-four hours.'

'Twenty-four! But I thought I would start at once!'

'Anyone suffering from jet-lag is useless to me. You missed a whole day *en route,* due to the time change, and I understand your flight took over twenty hours instead of the usual eighteen-and-a-half. You will go to your quarters right away and after unpacking you will go to bed and stay there. Meals will be served in your room. Whenever you waken, *if* you waken, you can ring for something, but I order you to get as much as twenty hours of consecutive rest. You may think you don't need it, but you'll be wrong. Hence the hard and fast rule that staff don't return to duty for twenty-four hours after flying from the U.K. Jet-lag impairs judgment *and* stamina. And don't imagine, if and when you waken, that you are refreshed enough to go walking or shopping. That's forbidden too. I don't want any doctor on the wards who isn't one hundred per cent ready for the job.'

He pressed a switch on his desk console and a moment later was saying, 'Doctor Freeman is with me, Matron. I have ordered her to get the usual amount of rest and would be obliged if you would make sure that she does. She seems a wilful young woman to me. It's up to you to tame her.'

CHAPTER THREE

The man was a tyrant. Inhuman. A bully who ordered her into purdah as if she were a female bought for his harem, though a man like that would prefer them as slaves, not mistresses! Diana turned her back on him and as she did so the door opened and in sailed Matron like a stalwart battleship.

'So there you are, Doctor Freeman— welcome to the Kinsale!' Shrewd eyes surveyed her sympathetically, then turned to the surgeon. 'Have you been bullying the girl?'

'*I*? I never bully! I have merely been instructing her for her own good,' Jonathan Kinsale snapped.

Matron murmured with a touch of irony, 'That's what I mean.' She threw Diana a glance which said all too eloquently, *Men*! Then she smiled. 'Come, my dear, you must be tired out. I'll take you along to your room myself, and then leave you in peace. I expect

Mr. Kinsale has been initiating you into the hospital rule about adequate sleep after prolonged flying, and I will endorse that, so you can forget about everything until you feel yourself again.'

'I don't feel not myself,' Diana protested feebly and ungrammatically as the door closed behind them. She had a brief glimpse of Jonathan Kinsale settling down to work, totally forgetful of her.

Matron said comfortably, 'Don't mind Mr. Kinsale, my dear. The truth is that being medical superintendent irks him. He would much rather be whole time at his real job, surgery. He is a very fine surgeon indeed.'

Diana could well believe that. To be a fine surgeon a man had to be cold, with nerves of steel. She could admire those qualities when at work, but outside it—couldn't he be a little more human? Other surgeons were. She knew from experience that surgeons were just as susceptible to women as doctors were. Training hospitals were full of them.

But at least Matron's welcome was warm, and she liked the woman's genial smile, her buxom motherliness—very unlike most hospital matrons, who all too often were starched and unbending and very much on their dignity. Matrons exerted more power in a hospital than people outside realised; few members of the medical staff, let alone the nursing staff, failed to be awed by them.

Matron's word could be law on all but actual doctoring and surgery, which meant that she could interfere in almost everything and very often did. She was the queen bee of the hive.

'If you've never been East before, Doctor, you will probably be a bit bewildered at first. Even homesick. So don't forget I'm here, will you? I've been at the Kinsale for twenty years and seen many doctors and nurses come and go. Few stay for ever. Hong Kong is known as the gateway to the East—travelling from the West, that is—and the gateway to the West coming back, which means there is a transitory quality about it, a sort of meeting place for East and West which makes it unlike anywhere else in the world. It truly *is* cosmopolitan in the fullest sense of the word. But it can be a bit overwhelming at first, so, as I say, don't forget I'm here if you need someone to talk to.'

She looked at the new young doctor compassionately. The girl might not realise it, but she looked all in. Rather more than jet-lag, I'd say, the woman reflected. I hope she has sufficient stamina to stand the pace of this hospital.

She said carefully, 'You do realise, don't you, that the Kinsale won't be a bit like your training hospital back home? I know St. Mark's—that's where you qualified, isn't it? A fine place, but it won't have prepared you for anything so unorthodox as this. We all have to pitch in wherever necessary at times. I have even acted as a ward sister when one has been off sick, and while we were without a house physician, Chris Muldoon had to help on Medical as well as Surgical, so don't be surprised if you're called for theatre duty in an emergency.'

'I should like it.'

'Good. In that event, you may even have a chance to see Mr. Kinsale at work.' She made it sound as if watching the Super at the operating table would be an honour bestowed by the gods.

'I'm sure that would be very interesting,' Diana answered politely.

Matron smiled a little. 'You've taken a dislike to him, haven't you?'

'I neither like nor dislike him, Matron. I am here to do a job, no more.'

The shrewd eyes looked satisfied. 'Good,' she said again. 'And here we are at your room. I thought you would like one with a view of the Peak and the harbour.' She opened a door and went ahead of Diana, crossing to a window directly opposite. Diana followed, coming to a halt beside the plump figure and, without realising that she did so, she gasped. Against a blue sky unflecked by any cloud towered the Peak of Hong Kong Island, and below lay the harbour, although all Diana could see of that was a far corner because the area immediately in front of her window was a maze of buildings. But even that distant glimpse of water was abuzz with activity; Chinese junks, ferry boats, sampans and ocean-going liners criss-crossed their way to and from the harbour mouth, and busy little tubs stuttered like water-borne bumble bees between the island and Kowloon.

'Those are walla-wallas,' Matron said, following her glance. 'In other words, water taxis. You find the view exciting? So do I. Even after all these years I find Hong Kong harbour the most stimulating in the world.' She turned at a tap on the door. 'Here comes an early supper for you. Forget about the view for now. Sustenance and then bed are what you need.'

A Chinese girl set down a tray and bowed low. 'Thank you, Ah,' Matron said, and the girl beamed from ear to ear, her tilted eyes almost disappearing, then padded off on noiseless feet.

'What did you call her, Matron?' Diana asked.

'Ah. Most amahs are called "Ah" because everyone has to have a title of some sort and "Ah" is a friendly non-Communist name. Amahs are female domestic help of all kinds, from baby-amahs to wash-amahs, but one would never insult them by even referring to them by the Cantonese term Gung-Yan, which means "work person" of both sexes, and in plural as well as singular, there being no actual word for "servant" in Cantonese.' Matron smiled. 'You won't find it bewildering in time.'

39

The woman patted Diana's arm comfortingly. 'My dear, you are going to be all right. I know it. I feel it. So you can forget Mr. Kinsale's intimidating manner. I know him well. It's a disguise, a front, no more.'

'Why should he need one?'

'You don't believe me? Well, I can't really blame you. I knew as soon as I entered his office that his reception hadn't been exactly warm. I'm afraid you mustn't expect that from him.'

'I have already come to that conclusion,' agreed Diana.

Matron seemed about to speak, then changed her mind. She walked to the door instead, then looked back.

'On the third Friday evening in every month—that will be this week, Doctor—I am at home to everyone from the rank of Sister upward, whether belonging to Medical, Surgical, or Admin. Six o'clock, for drinks. The secretary's office will direct you to my quarters. I look forward to seeing you then in a social capacity, but we will be sure to meet before that in the course of duty. Meanwhile, if you have any little problem or query, my office is at the end of the corridor between Medical and Surgical on the first floor, and I am always available between eight a.m. and ten a.m. before I inspect the wards.' Her motherly smile flashed again. 'Good luck, my dear. Good luck.'

And I'm going to need it, Diana thought. Oh, *how* I am going to need it! With the closing of the door and the exit of Matron's comforting personality, she felt forsaken, cut adrift, as if she had plunged headlong into alien waters without knowing how to navigate them.

And she was tired all through. She sank into a deep couch before the low table on which the amah had placed her tray. She even managed to swallow a little food, but far more tempting was the comfortable bed. She shed her clothes without knowing that she did so and slid naked between the sheets, lulled into instant oblivion by the shimmering heat of this February day and the hum of the air conditioner, but more than all by physical need, the like of which she had never experienced. Her last coherent thought was that the detestable Jonathan Kinsale had won the first round. She *did* need sleep. She felt as if she wanted to sleep for ever, never to wake up.

And for the first time in weeks, Clive's face, his memory and her need for him, didn't penetrate her consciousness even in dreams.

*   *   *

On the Friday following her arrival, Diana presented herself somewhat shyly at the door of Matron's apartment, which was situated on

41

the top floor. Only two other people had accommodation to equal hers—the medical secretary and his wife, and the chief almoner. The medical superintendent had a house in the grounds which set him apart exclusively from everyone, the resident surgical officer and chief house physician had their own bachelor flats, and so on down the hierarchy scale to Diana's level, which merited a comfortable room with a pleasant view and an amah shared with the chief dispenser, who was a woman, and two senior sisters, all of whom were accommodated on the same corridor. Male and female residential quarters were strictly apart.

Diana was a little awed by Matron's splendid apartment. Even when it was crowded with people she could see that it was spacious. The main living room had sliding windows from floor to ceiling. These opened on to a wide balcony which ran full length of the flat and was gaily adorned with tubs of flowers and luxurious garden furniture.

An obsequious amah conducted Diana out to the balcony, where Matron, surprisingly magnificent out of uniform, was receiving her guests. She wore a voluminous gown of trailing grey chiffon which made her look like an elephant draped in cobwebs, and a very regal elephant at that. A discreet brooch of sapphires was pinned on the left shoulder, and matching jewels adorned her ears and fingers.

42

Diana was to learn that Hong Kong was one of the trading centres of the world as far as jewellery was concerned, as well as in most other things.

'Well, Doctor, and how are you settling down?' Matron asked, drawing her into a group beside the balcony rail.

'Quite well, I think. At least, I hope so.'

'Don't be modest, my dear. I have heard no complaints from either staff or patients.'

No complaints, perhaps, but no praise either. Diana knew well enough that she was on probation and that to survive the first weeks without too much criticism would be an achievement.

'And my own observation is pretty reliable,' Matron was continuing, 'but you're not here to be vetted, so let us forget work and introduce you to everyone. Lady Collard, let me present our new junior house physician, newly arrived from London. Lady Collard, my dear, is the wife of our Colonial Secretary. Hong Kong, as you know, is still a British Crown Colony—'

'And long may it remain so,' said a high-toned male voice. 'Even if China reclaims the New Territories when the lease expires, both East and West need the trade freedom which Hong Kong represents under the present *status quo.*'

'You, a Chinese, say that, Doctor Chang?'

'I and many Chinese say that.'

Diana looked at the man whose hand was

now extended to her. 'Doctor Chang—Doctor Freeman—' Matron's voice was intoning. 'Doctor Chang's daughter is a staff nurse here. You will have already met her, I'm sure.'

'The pretty girl on Lotus? Indeed I have.' Diana remembered the friendly girl who had brought tea to the Super's office. 'I heard Sister Lotus praising her only the other day and saying she should go far.'

A woman's voice remarked, 'I fancy she will marry before that. My daughter was never intended solely for a hospital career, any more than I was.'

'My wife, Barbara,' Dr. Chang presented the woman with an affectionate pride which was fully justified. Barbara Chang was a pretty woman in her fifties, with bright intelligent eyes and a contented expression.

'And this is Dr. Kinsale,' Matron announced. 'He has been looking forward to meeting you.'

A white-haired man with a kindly smile held out his hand. 'I have been looking forward to meeting her *again,* Matron. Although I was her fellow-passenger all the way from London, it wasn't until the final moments of the flight that we exchanged more than a few words.'

Diana was surprised to see the elderly gentleman whom she had last seen as they touched down at Kai Tak, but even more surprised to learn his name.

'Kinsale?' she echoed. 'So you are

44

connected with the hospital! Why didn't you tell me?'

'I scarcely had time, my dear.' He drew her away to a far corner of the balcony. Above them spread a striped awning, and below lay the whole expanse of the harbour. Matron certainly had a superb view. Diana found a glass in her hand, the contents of which she sipped absently. She was more than delighted to meet this nice old gentleman again, even though he was apparently related—distantly, surely?—to the detestable Jonathan Kinsale.

'I am not connected with the medical side of the hospital since my retirement,' he was saying, 'but I remain as chairman of the hospital board. And now here comes my son, whom you have met, of course.'

The *Super,* son of this charming old man? Diana had difficulty in disguising her astonishment as Jonathan Kinsale gave her a cool nod and greeted his father with the comment that since he appeared to have met Doctor Freeman he need not trouble to introduce her. The next moment he had drifted away, his father watching him thoughtfully. Then the older man turned back to Diana, saying conversationally, 'I don't suppose you've had time to do much exploring yet, so let me point out some places of interest.'

He turned and looked out across the water, and Diana did likewise, only too glad to turn

45

her back on the crowd and in particular on Jonathan Kinsale.

'Let's dispense with formality, shall we? I am Hammond to everyone—Hammond Kinsale, a retired physician and everyone's friend, which means that I hope to be yours also, Doctor Diana. Oh yes, I know your Christian name and have every intention of using it. Formality can be chilling and there is no place for it in a small community like ours.'

You should tell that to your son, she thought wryly, marvelling that so warm and friendly a person as this could have fathered a man so remote and chilling as Jonathan Kinsale.

'Tell me about Hong Kong,' she said, 'I know so little. Only that it is divided into two parts, the island and Kowloon Peninsula—'

'Plus the new territories, which are held on a ninety-nine year lease from China. It expires in 1997. We have developed those territories superbly, so they will obviously be reclaimed, to China's advantage, when the time comes. You must explore the New Territories while you are still able to move about them freely.'

'And what about this view?' she said appreciatively. 'Never did I dream that I would one day stand on a a balcony gazing down on the South China Seas!'

'Beautiful, isn't it?' the old man smiled. 'Of course, having been born here, it seems especially lovely to me, though the changes even in my time have been so rapid as to be

46

almost incredible. You are looking across to Hong Kong Island—that skyscraper district is Victoria, capital of the colony, but more commonly known as Central District. The Kowloon Peninsula is always referred to locally as Kowloon side, and the island as Hong Kong side. The name Hong Kong is derived from "Heung Gong", meaning "Fragrant Harbour", which was the Chinese name for an anchorage at the floating village of Aberdeen. The anchorage was so named because ships could take on fresh water from a spring nearby.'

'And "Kowloon"— where does that come from?'

'That is even more interesting. The name means "Nine Dragons"— "Kow" for nine and "Loon" for dragons. Eight hundred years ago, when the boy Emperor Ping counted eight hills here, he remarked that there must be eight dragons, because of the belief that a dragon inhabits every mountain. His prime minister told him that there were nine dragons, because of another ancient belief that emperors were dragons also.'

'And the business sector of Kowloon is called Tsim Sha Tsui.'

'You pronounce that well. If in the whirl of your busy life you ever have time to study Chinese names and derivations, you will be fascinated—and you'll find the Chinese calendar an essential study, otherwise you will be bewildered by so many celebrations. Throughout the year you will see celebrations for Buddha's Birthday, Dragon Boat Day— that is a sight worth seeing—the Bun Festival, the Maiden's Festival, Hungry Ghosts Day and the Chung Yeung Festival, until the Chinese New Year comes round again. At that time they give gifts of "lai see" money to family and friends, in bright red envelopes with "Kung Hei Fat Choy" in gold Chinese lettering, which means roughly, "Happy New Year", but more literally "make lots of money"— both the "lai see" money and the red envelopes are to bring good luck. Ah, now the lights are springing up on the island! Isn't it a lovely sight?'

Diana nodded, entranced. It seemed as if the whole of Hong Kong side was rising like stars into the dusky evening sky, with the Peak as its crowning glory.

Dusk gave way to darkness swiftly and early in these parts, and for a while they gazed in silence. At one point a thousand neon lights already blazed.

'That is the Wanchai district,' Hammond told her, 'better known as The World of Suzy Wong. Films and novels have immortalised this colony, and not only through Suzy. Had you seen the opening shots of *Love Is A Many-Splendoured Thing* you would have been prepared for our incredible descent between the mountains of Kowloon and across the harbour to Kai Tak airport. But I am

48

monopolizing you, my dear. I see Chris Muldoon watching you from over there, and that son of mine will grow impatient if I keep him waiting—he has time only for a quick dinner tonight before going on duty again. As I thought, he is coming across to remind me . . .'

Seconds later, Chris was also beside them, but he had to wait before Diana noticed him. She was watching Jonathan Kinsale leaving with his father, and her expression was thoughtful.

'Fallen for the man?' Chris teased. 'If so, you'll be in the fashion. I believe there isn't a woman on the hospital staff, let alone amongst the patients, who isn't head over heels in love with the Super.'

'You surprise me,' she said, and meant it. How could any woman fall in love with a man like that? He had bidden her no more than a curt goodnight before carrying his father away. 'What surprises me still more is that those two men are even related,' she added.

Chris had to admit that they weren't much alike. 'He's a great guy, isn't he, old Hammond? But don't be taken in by his son's manner. Many men need to wear a mask.'

'Do you?'

He grinned. 'Not yet, but if I ever reach Kinsale's position maybe I'll be glad to. At the present moment I'm not well-heeled enough to be the target for ambitious women or match-making mums.'

49

'Neither of whom get very far with Mr. Kinsale, I imagine.'

Chris shrugged.

'From all accounts, some woman did at some time or other, but that's his concern and not mine. My concern right now is to grab a quick meal with you as company. How about it? We're both due back on duty at nine-thirty, so let's make the most of our out-of-school time.'

His hand was beneath her elbow, propelling her towards Matron. 'Say your party piece like a good girl—"thank you for having me" and all that jazz—then it's the Jade Garden and a bowl of shark's fin soup, followed by dim sum. What's dim sum? I'll tell you when we've said goodnight to our hostess. *Good*night, Matron!' He bowed over the plump, beringed hand. 'As usual, your hospitality has lightened the life of two hard-working medicos—what would we poor slaves of the Kinsale do without your beneficient presence?'

'Chris Muldoon, you've drunk too much, as usual.' Matron was laughing, indulgence in her face and in her voice. 'Take him somewhere and stoke him with food to sober him, Dr. Freeman. Goodnight, my dear—no need for thanks. I am only sorry dear Hammond monopolized you, because Mr. Wong was waiting to be introduced. That means *you* must wait now, Mr. Muldoon—'

Chris stepped aside while Matron drew a

dapper Chinese forward. 'Mr. Lee Wong and his wife Mae. Mr. Wong handles the hospital's legal affairs.'

Diana's face lit up. 'Pearl's brother! She said we would meet sooner or later—'

'It would have been sooner,' said Mae Wong, 'had my husband not been tied up with a court case. The Supreme Court here is very demanding—as demanding as the Kinsale Hospital is toward its medical staff, I believe.'

Mae Wong was an enchanting creature, diminutive as a doll and slender as a willow. Like many cosseted oriental wives, she seemed too youthful to be the mother of six small children, about whom Diana had already heard.

The usual pleasantries were exchanged, the usual greetings and polite enquiries as to how much free time she was likely to have and when she would be available to visit their home? Then Lee Wong lowered his voice. 'If you would be so kind as to report on my sister's behaviour, Doctor, every member of our family, which is as extensive as most Chinese families are, would appreciate it. Pearl belongs to this generation and doesn't cherish our ancient beliefs in the way that the Wongs do.'

'But there is nothing wrong with Pearl's behaviour!' Diana protested. 'She works hard at her job, which is an exacting one, and outside it she is decorum itself. As a flatmate I couldn't have asked for anyone better.'

Lee Wong's smooth, inscrutable face looked as satisfied as he could make it, but already Diana was learning that the Chinese countenance was difficult to read. There was something about the unlined, ageless quality of it which made it sometimes seem like a mask.

'I find your words reassuring, Doctor, and hope they are justified.'

'Of course they are,' Diana declared, bewildered.

'But tell me—how did she behave when not with you?'

Mae Wong interrupted, 'My dear husband, what a foolish question! How could Doctor Freeman possibly know how Pearl behaved when out of her sight?' The enchanting creature turned to Diana. 'I feel I should explain. Rumours have reached my husband that his naughty young sister has been seen around London with a man who is what you would call "off-beat". We conventional Chinese do not like off-beat manners or behaviour. I fear dear Pearl, the youngest member of the Wong family and educated in the States, has possibly been over-indulged. She returned from America with a very independent mind. That shocked our Chinese elders, who find it hard to accept such a thing in women.'

'In Pearl's case I would call it self-reliance rather than independence,' Diana said. 'Her job demands it. For this reason you have nothing to worry about, Mr. Wong.'

The conversation ended there, and only then was Chris able to carry Diana away.

'Pin a medal on me for waiting so long,' he said. 'I'm damned hungry and ready for more than shark's fin soup and dim sum, but we'll have plenty of that before the curfew falls on our sparse off-duty time. Dim sum, fair Diana, is just about the quickest and most appetising Chinese meal you can get. It also happens to be one of the cheapest—a consideration to mere housemen. A waitress comes round with covered baskets containing portions of crab, sho'mai, spring roll, and every other sort of delicacy. You might find the odd bit of snake thrown in, though that's a gourmet touch mostly reserved for more costly menus. Anyway, you just eat what you want and as much as you want and at the end your empty baskets are counted up, and that's that. In other words, you pay only for the empties! Here we are at the Jade Garden and I hope your appetite is as hearty as mine.'

To her surprise, because she seemed to have given little thought to food since her arrival in Hong Kong, Diana found that it was.

*   *   *

'It would have been a friendly gesture to invite young Doctor Freeman to dine with us,'

Hammond Kinsale remarked to his son as they drove away.

'But unnecessary. Muldoon had the same idea.'

'So you noticed that you did?' The old man glanced at Jonathan quizzically, silently reflecting that this was a good sign. Not since that mess-up with Gloria had his son paid any heed to women, and that miserable affair could have been tidied up long ago.

'Did I hear you tell Matron that you had already met Diana Freeman?' Jonathan asked as he headed for the new tunnel beneath the harbour which linked Kowloon side with the island. 'When did it happen?'

'On my way home from visiting your Aunt Katherine in London. We sat next to each other on the flight, but she gave me no chance to exchange more than a few words.'

'So you weren't travelling first class? I can't understand why you deny yourself essential comforts when you can so easily afford them?'

'I have more than essential comfort at home. There, I deny myself nothing. And I find it no hardship to travel with the rest of the human race rather than with expense-account tycoons, who unfailingly jar on me.' Hammond finished good-naturedly, 'Let me live my own life in my own way, Jonathan.'

'Could I do otherwise?' His son smiled at him, then turned his attention back to the road. Emerging from the tunnel they skirted

54

the waterfront at Wanchai, heading toward the flyover and the area of City Hall and Star Ferry, then veering off Connaught Road Central and up Cotton Tree Drive to the Mid-Levels, the most sought-after part of the Peak district because it escaped the mist and humidity which hung almost perpetually over the Peak itself and corroded everything from furniture to properties. On the Mid-Levels, apartments and villas enjoyed the lovely views which were all too frequently blotted out from the Peak, with the added advantage of accessibility to business and shopping areas of the island, but well above traffic noises.

Jonathan had to concede that as far as home comforts were concerned, the old man denied himself nothing, which was as it should be after his years of devotion to the hospital, a devotion which continued. After his wife's death during Jonathan's early youth, Hammond's whole life had been dedicated to two things—the Kinsale, and his son's career. In neither, Jonathan hoped, had he been disappointed, except in the matter of his son's misguided engagement, but that was something to which they rarely referred.

'We could dine in the Mandarin Grill,' Jonathan suggested, but his father shook his head.

'One should never hurry over a meal at the Mandarin, and since you have to be on duty again shortly let's enjoy it at my place. I

55

ordered dinner before leaving, so there'll be no delay.'

The luxury block where Hammond lived was a well-known one called Luginsland. His penthouse had a roof garden which was one of the joys of his life. The fragrance of heliotrope and mimosa and frangipani drifted from enormous tubs and stone troughs. Giant branches of eucalyptus and rubber plant climbed the walls of an arbour, over which morning glory had been trained to form a canopy. Sitting out here was like sitting in a garden half way between earth and sky, and after an excellent meal, waited on by Hammond's well-trained manservant, the two men sat back and relaxed, brandy and cigars to hand. In the distance, just left of the Kowloon side of Star Ferry, the rooftop of the hospital could be seen.

'Tell me about Diana Freeman,' Hammond urged.

'What about her?' Jonathan asked warily.

'All you know. Not merely that she's attractive. I can see that for myself.'

'Attractive? I hadn't noticed.'

'More's the pity. When are you going to stop shunning women just because Gloria let you down? In this day and age a man in your position would have no qualms about looking elsewhere—in any day and age, for that matter. You should stop judging other women by her unreliable standards. This once-bitten-

56

twice-shy stuff is ridiculous and cowardly.'

'Cowardly!' exclaimed his son.

'What else? You are wasting your life and your manhood.'

'Not my life, at least. I hope the hospital justifies that.'

'I'm sorry,' Hammond said quickly. 'I spoke without thought, but only because I do hate waste. You are thirty-eight now, and because of one mistake you deny yourself all possibility of a happy marriage. As far as I know, you don't even form associations with women any more, though there was a time—'

'I leave amorous adventures to men like Chris Muldoon.'

'Who seemed intent, this evening, on getting Diana to himself.'

'Why shouldn't he? He is conscientious over his work so deserves some light relief now and then.'

'Which he can get in every form in Hong Kong—'

'Providing he can afford it. A man pays through the nosc at most places catering for male amusement, and Escort girls are even more pricey.'

'You speak from experience?' enquired Hammond.

'Of course. I've tried them occasionally, but not for a long time now. Even the nicer ones palled—and there are quite a lot of very nice girls on the books of the Alliance and Escort agencies.'

'They can be no substitute for personal relationships, of course.'

'If one wants personal relationships, which I don't,' Jonathan said curtly.

'There *are* other things besides work—'

'Which I am content to leave to other people. You made the hospital your life, Father, so why shouldn't I? As you said earlier, let me live my own life in my own way.'

'*Touché.*' His father laughed and gave up. He knew full well that to lecture his son about his private life was a waste of time, but he had been unable to resist the opportunity tonight because he had been pleased that Jonathan had noticed Muldoon's attention to Diana. He took that to be a good sign, and even hoped it might indicate a possible thaw, but he was wise enough to know when to keep silent.

But before they parted he couldn't resist one final comment. 'By the way, do you know that Diana Freeman is unhappy?'

Jonathan Kinsale gave a slight shrug.

'I can't imagine why you should think that. She looked happy enough this evening.'

'In company, yes, with champagne flowing. Matron is always liberal with the champagne, having laid in stocks when the price was even lower than it is now in Hong Kong. Don't be deceived by false gaiety, my son. Look in the girl's eyes. There's a withdrawn sort of expression about them. A hurt look. I feel

58

sorry for her. So might you, if you studied her. Properly, I mean, and without prejudice.'

Jonathan Kinsale threw his father a glance which said all too plainly that he had no intention of doing that.

CHAPTER FOUR

Staff Nurse Chang tapped respectfully on the door of Matron's office, waited for her summons, and entered. 'Is Dr. Freeman here, please, Matron?'

'No, Staff. I expect she's on the wards just now.'

'Will I do?' Chris Muldoon asked. He was studying some case papers over Matron's shoulder. 'Something urgent?'

'It's Elisha again.'

'Good lord, has *he* come back?'

'He always does,' said Matron, 'and always will so long as the authorities allow him to remain in Hong Kong. This hospital is a second home to him. In fact,' she finished sadly, 'I suspect it's about the only home he has now, poor old man.'

'When was he brought in?' Chris asked.

'He wasn't,' said Staff Nurse Chang. 'He just wandered in half an hour ago and collapsed in Outpatients. Dr. Freeman is on duty and Sister Casualty asked me to find her.'

Matron flicked a switch on her desk console and said into a microphone, 'Call Dr. Freeman to Casualty, please.' To Dorothy she nodded. 'All right, Staff—she's being bleeped right away.'

'Thank you, Matron.'

Half way along the corridor outside, Chris Muldoon overtook Dr. Chang's daughter.

'And how's my little Lotus Blossom?'

'Not yours, sir.'

He gave a mock sigh. 'Will you ever be?'

May you never know how much I'd like to be, Dorothy thought, but aloud she answered negligently, 'With all the women in your life, you can do without one more. Especially with that glamour girl from Government House around.'

'Estelle? Alas, she isn't around any more. She took herself out of my life, voluntarily. She disliked being neglected in favour of a lady doctor.'

'Doctor Diana, you mean?'

Chris grinned. 'Is that what you call her?'

'It's what everyone calls her, staff and patients as well. I must say I can hardly blame Estelle. Doctor Diana could be quite a rival.'

'If she thawed a little, yes, but chipping the icicles off her is proving a mammoth job. I wooed her at the Jade Garden after Matron's shindig last week, entirely without success. She was more interested in the dim sum than in me.'

'After the hours she puts in, who can blame her? Have you ever tried to calculate how many miles a house physician covers when on duty? Not to mention the nurses? Considerably more than surgical staff.'

'So you're on her side?'

'Of course. As for her icicles, you wouldn't suspect she had any if you saw her with the patients. Especially children.'

'The nice thing about you, Lotus Blossom, is the way you stick up for your own sex. I've never heard you bitch another member of it, which is more than I can say for Estelle.'

'And who is filling *her* gap in your life?' asked Dorothy.

'There's a vacancy at the moment. Care to apply?'

'No time.'

'Too many dates, too many other men?'

Let him think so, Dorothy decided, even though it isn't true. Pretend they're queueing up at the door of the Nurses' Home . . .

But her honesty prevented that. Everyone knew that nurses at the Kinsale had precious little free time, dividing their lives between the wards and their three-bedded dormitories, with a few snatched hours of shopping or a quick swim at Shek-O Beach or Deepwater Bay, or a half-day on Lantao Island or, in her case, a visit to her parents. So why pretend?

'You know the routine, Chris. It's yours as well, except that as a man you can chat up a girl in the Peninsula Lobby—'

'Never there! The Peninsula is too grand for pick-ups.'

'Other places, then, where a nurse can't or won't go. Despite the social freedom of Hong Kong, it only applies to men or call girls. There's no women's lib here for the likes of us. We'd lose our jobs at the Kinsale if we stepped over the border, and what is there to step into on the other side? Only the topless bars and the strip clubs.'

He frowned distastefully. 'Not for the likes of you, Lotus Blossom. But remember, there *are* men on the hospital staff. Think of all the romances there have been between doctors and nurses here. They found time to fit them in somehow.'

She laughed and turned aside. They had reached Outpatients by now. She nodded goodbye, wishing he would find time to fit in a romance with her, and hoping he would never guess how much she wished for it.

'I'll take a look at Elisha,' he said, making it an excuse to follow her. Dorothy didn't stop him, even though it was Dr. Diana, and not he, who had been called there.

*   *   *

Diana's summons, bleeping from the battery-operated call device in the breast pocket of her white overall, had brought her to Outpatients quickly, and when Chris and Dorothy entered she was already stooping over the patient. He was old and almost in the last stages of exhaustion.

'He'll be all right,' she said over her shoulder, 'providing he has plenty of rest and nourishment.'

'That need always brings him here,' Chris said, 'and as you've probably observed, he isn't the only one. Well, if there's nothing I can do, I'll be on my way.' With a cheerful grin at Dorothy Chang and an airy wave to Diana, he was gone.

Diana stood for a moment, looking down at the old man. There was little flesh on him and the skin of his face sagged loosely from finely chiselled features. She took the chart Sister Casualty had handed over to her, and studied it.

'Doesn't anyone know who he is, Staff?'

To her surprise, Jonathan Kinsale's voice answered.

'We call him Elisha. With that flowing beard and mane he looks like a Biblical prophet, don't you agree? He forgot his own name years ago—or so he says. Personally, I suspect that was from choice.' He looked at the old man with compassion. 'I heard he was back, and wanted to see him for myself. Not that there is anything we can do beyond feeding him and resting him and sending him out to his obscure life again.'

'But what is an Englishman doing in this state, in Hong Kong of all places? It's a British Protectorate. He could seek help.'

'I suspect that pride won't let him. Or fear, perhaps. He probably knows that he would be sent back to England for his own good. But it wouldn't be *his* idea of what is good for him.'

'You mean he would rather struggle on here, than be looked after at home?' demanded Diana.

'Something like that. And he isn't the only one. Hong Kong gets in the blood. Apart from the usual run of accidents to tourists and visitors and residents, a large percentage of our patients are more or less regulars. I have some interesting case histories on file, if you'd care to see them.'

She accepted at once, and went along with him to his office. It was the first time she had visited this room since the day of her arrival and as she entered, the scene returned to her vividly. He had made it plain that he didn't want her here, yet now he was opening a filing cabinet and placing case histories before her.

'Take Elisha—all we know of him is that he is some sort of an artist, but what kind we haven't yet been able to find out. Whether he was a commercial or a fine-art painter would help us to establish his identity; if the former, he would have worked for some organisation; if the latter, that would be less easy. He must have come to the colony years ago, because he is very skilled at covering his traces when he's eventually discharged. He probably moves from one squalid room to another, kicked out when he fails to pay the rent, poor devil.'

'Sister got an address from him this time, just before he passed out.'

'That's something, but the chances are that he's been evicted and his possessions, such as they are, taken in lieu of rent.'

'But surely he could apply for some sort of aid?'

Jonathan Kinsale shrugged. 'He could, but men like Elisha are too proud to accept charity, which is how he regards the very good welfare services in operation. I suspect he shuns them for other reasons, and one particularly—that as a British subject his welfare would consist of being sent back home, to a country which is no longer home to him. Only Hong Kong is that. Here is another case—' He pushed a folder across his desk and, curiously, Diana opened it. The records concerned a Yorkshireman who had come to the colony as a youth, working in a travel agency. The agency closed down and the young man drifted from job to job, never really getting anywhere but perfectly happy so long as he could remain in Hong Kong.

'Rather obscurity here than success elsewhere, that sums up his case,' the Super told her. 'Eventually he grew old, ill health dogged him, and he came to the Kinsale. That was when my father was superintendent. The almoner contacted Government House, and their welfare department contacted his relatives in England, who proved to be far from well-off and unable to raise his fare home. As soon as he was fit to travel, it was paid for him at this end and everyone presumed they had seen the last of him. Not so. Eventually he landed a job in the galley of a ship heading for Hong Kong, and disappeared ashore as soon as it docked at Ocean Terminal. And no matter how many times he fell flat on his face financially and was transported home, he always managed to return. Eventually, at a ripe old age, he died happily in the Kinsale.'

Diana picked up another file, and read more or less the same story. Many concerned impoverished English widows, existing on meagre pensions which became less and less adequate.

'You'll see them in places like the Peninsula or Mandarin lobbies,' Jonathan told her. 'Not because they live there, they couldn't afford to, but because they are fashionable places which they have always patronized. Habits die hard, even when people are in reduced circumstances, but they can turn their backs on rented rooms for a few hours each day, making a pot of tea or coffee span the hours between a lonely morning and a lonely evening, and being greeted by the hotel managements with courtesy and respect. They are always scrupulously groomed, even if their clothes are no longer fashionable. They keep the ragged banners of their pride flying this way, and their memories alive. They still *belong* to Hong Kong, which is important to them. It's difficult to make new friends in old age, and roots which have gone deep are hard to dig up and transplant into soil which has become alien over the years. When illness finally brings them to us, our job is not to criticize, but to help.'

'But these young ones?' Diana glanced through a thick sheaf.

'Ah, the young ones! They are the biggest problem. The elderly we can help and care for, but the young ones won't let us; girls who have come out here as governesses, or as members of dancing troupes or cabarets; as companions or secretaries, even. Hong Kong ensnares them just as badly. The longer you work here, the more surprised you'll be by the number of girls, of all nationalities, who drift here and refuse to ever drift away again. They fill the clubs, the discotheques, and even the massage parlours eventually, until they are too old to attract men any more.'

'And after that?'

Jonathan's shoulders rose and fell in a shrug which was far from indifferent. There was despair in it, but pity too.

'After that, if they are lucky, they get jobs in

67

cash desks, or as receptionists taking bookings. That is the tragic side of Hong Kong, but *not* the predominant. The Escort girls, for instance, enjoy life very much. Many are highly paid, and deserve to be. They are well educated, good conversationalists, well versed in politics and current affairs, even in financial and commercial matters, and all speak several languages fluently. They have to be elegant and good-looking and refined and, above all, good listeners. They are hired to be a tired businessman's companion for an evening, no more, but when the evening is over an escort girl can spend as long as she likes with a man if he appeals to her, and no questions asked. If he doesn't appeal, he can bring no pressure to bear beyond the hours booked and paid for in advance at a very high fee. If he tried to, the agencies would black-list him. These girls know how to look after themselves and a man knows they are companioning him only professionally. For my money, there's something unsatisfatory about bought companionship.'

(For *your* money? That means you've tried them yourself). Diana began to look at this man from a different viewpoint. Could it be possible that he was lonely?

Jonathan gathered up the files and put them away, saying briskly, 'It was for people such as old Elisha that the Kinsale was originally established. *Then* it was intended for British

68

and Colonial patients only, but so long as there's a vacant bed we never refuse help to any ailing person. Our maternity ward, for instance, has become extremely popular with Hong Kong Chinese. Some families won't allow their womenfolk to have their babies anywhere else. Families like the Yengtohs—'

'The couture people?'

He nodded. 'Goodness knows how many Yengtoh babies have been born here. I understand they show their gratitude by letting the staff have special terms. Matron will tell you about that. I opposed the idea when it was discovered. Our job is to care for people's health, irrespective of whether they can repay or not, and certainly not to expect privileges in return. However,' he gave that characteristic shrug again, 'it's not for me to interfere with female schemes, and if they help our underpaid nurses, then I see virtue in them. You may have learned already that our nurses are all State Registered in England, and could therefore command much higher salaries elsewhere. There are no probationers here, so the standard of nursing is high. It is my resolve that the medical attention shall always be of the highest, too.'

That, she thought, was ensured under a medical superintendent such as he.

To her surprise, he asked how she was settling down. 'Well, I hope?' For a man who didn't want her around that was rather big of him, she thought, and smiled in spite of herself. The Super looked at her with interest. When she smiled she was quite lovely. Even he, determined misogynist though he was, noticed that. Could his father's verdict on this girl be right? Was she really something more than an efficient young woman in a white overall?

'And how do you like Hong Kong?' he asked.

'I've had little chance to explore it yet.'

To her surprise, the touch of irony in her voice made him laugh, and his whole face changed. The sternness, the reserve, the aloofness vanished. Something within Diana stirred in response, and for the first time since she had parted from Clive, she felt a flicker of warmth in her heart.

'Then we must rectify that, Doctor. I'm sorry you have been so slave-driven since your arrival.'

'I am not sorry, sir. Work is what I came for.'

He gave her an intent look which she could not interpret. She was unaware that he heard an echo of his father's voice saying, *Take a good look at her . . . A proper look, I mean. And without prejudice.* What he saw now made him want to go on looking at her for a long time.

He jerked away and opened the door for her. As she passed through he saw a highlight in her hair, emphasizing its brilliance. A lovely

70

colour, he thought, and let his eyes linger on it. Lovely to look at and lovely to touch. He had an impulse to do so, but managed to check it. Instead, he watched her disappear down the corridor, then went back to his office.

For a while he stood looking through the window. He could see the distant rooftops of the City Hall Centre and reflected idly that preparations must already be under way there for the annual Hong Kong Arts Festival, in which the world's leading orchestras, conductors, and musicians performed, also leading theatrical and ballet companies. He had not yet glanced at the Festival programme, though a copy had arrived on his desk, but he made a mental note to get his usual quota of tickets to take his father and other guests. The Arts Festival was one of the few occasions when he permitted himself to take time off from the hospital.

He found himself wondering whether Diana Freeman liked classical music, as he did, or whether she preferred drama and ballet. The speculation surprised him so much that he turned away from the window abruptly and forced himself to work.

And how long was it since force had been necessary for that?

CHAPTER FIVE

Diana's sudden release from duty that afternoon took her by surprise. Chris Muldoon burst into the doctors' common room and pointed an accusing finger at her.

'For this, fair Diana, I shall never forgive you! Twice in one month I have been forced to break a date because of you. The first time finished me with Estelle, and now the same thing is likely to happen with a girl I've been trying to date ever since I saw her at the Peninsula's New Year Eggnog jamboree—'

'Their *what* jamboree?' she asked, laughing.

'Eggnog and cocktails at the Peninsula—it's traditional on the morning of New Year's Day, from eleven to twelve-thirty. All Hong Kong society crowds in, plus every ambassadorial head and every celebrated visitor. This year, Mimi du Cros stood out a mile. I saw her standing alone on that grand staircase, but by the time I managed to fight my way to her side a portly old gent had got there before me—the French Consul, no less.'

'And what has all this to do with me?'

'You threaten a promising relationship by making me break my first date with her! It has taken me all of two months to wangle an introduction—she's the Consul's personal secretary, no less, and French Consulate staff are protected by social barricades—'

'—which you obviously succeeded in breaking through.'

'Not without difficulty. And with even greater difficulty I managed to persuade her to dine with me. Tonight. And now *you* put a spoke in the wheel by swopping your duty with mine, which means I'll have to break our date. I'd very much like to know how you pulled *that* fast one. I don't suppose Mimi, any more than Estelle, will enjoy being stood up for a woman doctor—or for any woman, if it comes to that.'

'If I knew what you were talking about, I'd follow you better. Suppose you go back to the beginning?'

'The beginning,' he said with mock severity, 'was at Kai Tak Airport, when your late arrival caused me to miss my date with Estelle. She waited in the Den at the Hilton for a full hour, or so she said, though I'd guess a quarter was more true. Estelle was never a girl to hang around for any man, and after that little fiasco she told me so in no mean terms.'

'Then you're well rid of her,' Diana retorted. 'Furthermore, I didn't ask to be met, nor was I responsible for the plane being late.'

He acknowledged that, but was still slightly aggrieved. 'If only you had come to *me* instead of going to the Super! *He* doesn't fix the duty rota. Why didn't you just *ask* me to swop with you? Not that I would have agreed, of course, having waited so long for a date with Mimi.

But to be told abruptly, as I was today, that Dr. Freeman has been kept at the grindstone too much since her arrival and must therefore be given immediate time off— that's a bit much!'

'Chris Muldoon, I know nothing of this! I haven't asked for any duty release. As far as I'm concerned, I'm on duty until ten tonight.'

'Incorrect. *I* am on duty until ten tonight. An order from Kinsale not half an hour ago, as we left the theatre, though I must admit he didn't rap it out exactly like that. He put it more cunningly; said he was disturbed to learn that you'd not even had time to look around Hong Kong since your arrival, so he was sure I wouldn't mind taking your duty for the rest of the day. "She needs some fresh air, Muldoon. She's looking pale . . ." That nearly knocked me sideways, I can tell you. It's the first time I've ever heard Kinsale comment on a woman's looks, much less show concern for them. It seems you've been using your feminine wiles to my disadvantage.'

Across the room the R.S.O., hitherto submerged in the *Hong Kong Standard*, gave a shout of laughter.

'Congratulations, Diana! You seem to have ousted this young man as no member of the medical staff has ever been able to.'

'Not deliberately. And of course, I'll stick to the rota as arranged, Chris.'

'That you won't. When the Great White Chief commands, his subjects obey. You'll learn that in time, if you haven't already.' The house surgeon's good-natured face surveyed her without rancour. 'Run along and get that fresh air—you've earned it. And perhaps playing hard to get won't queer my pitch with Mimi after all.'

'If it does, you won't have to look far for a replacement. There are pretty girls in this hospital, if you take the trouble to look.'

And I could name one in particular, she thought, remembering Dorothy Chang's obvious interest in him. All the same, she was sorry for spoiling Chris's evening, and said so.

'Don't be sorry,' advised the R.S.O., 'Muldoon's heart is resilient. And if you like,' he finished with a wry grin in Chris's direction, 'I'll act as stand-in for you. Where did you say you were meeting this girl?'

'I didn't. Nor am I going to. Pick your own women, Maynard.'

*　　　*　　　*

Diana was touched by the Super's unexpected thought. What a contradiction the man was—a man who could send tea along to a nervous newcomer, then tell her pointblank that he didn't want her around; a man who could be brisk and cold and businesslike, then compassionate toward a patient who couldn't remember his own name; a man who could drive his staff mercilessly, then, without

75

warning, release them from duty because they were looking pale . . .

He was an enigma she would never understand, and as she went up to her room to change, as she showered and made up her face and slipped into a cool cotton dress, as she left the hospital and walked across Kowloon Park into Nathan Road and then strolled among the shops, she found her mind totally occupied with Jonathan Kinsale—and that puzzled her, too. She didn't like the man, so to find herself thinking about him was inexplicable.

Turning in her tracks, she made her way by Peking Road into Canton Road and then turned right to the Ocean Terminal, a vast shopping complex flanking the Star Ferry and the harbour. Ocean-going liners of every nationality were berthed. From the roof of the complex she looked down on endless rows of them—Russian, Dutch, American, Rumanian, Greek, British, Japanese; the flags of all nations proclaimed this to be a multi-national port of endless fascination, and she stayed up there, relishing the warm breezes off the South China Seas, until the first signs of dusk appeared and lights began to spring up amongst the high-rise buildings of Victoria and amongst the lower roofs of Kowloon side, then she descended to the shopping complex, where stores still stood open, selling fashions, jewellery, ivories and jade, fine leather goods and Chinese crafts—and paintings which reminded her of Clive's work.

Some of his best stage sets were those which he had created for shows like *Lady Precious Stream, Madam Butterfly,* and oriental ballets. He had once been taught by a man who imbued into his pupils an appreciation of oriental art, and some of this appreciation Clive had passed on to her, so that she lingered now before the open door of a shop filled with Chinese hand-painted screens, wishing that Clive were with her to admire them.

There she was, thinking about him again— remembering, remembering, remembering. Recalling the first time he took her along to his studio off the Fulham Road, an almost derelict warehouse which he had bought because it was big enough in which to produce scenery on a vast scale. That was the first time he had taken her in his arms and kissed her. 'Right in the middle of a Chinese garden,' he had pointed out tenderly, teasingly. 'I hope you like being made love to on the set for a revival of *Chu Chin Chow*?'

'I'd like it anywhere, anywhere at all!' And his lovemaking after that had been uncontrolled.

With an effort, she jerked back to the moment, to the crowded shopping arcade and the multitude of oriental and Western faces milling about her. With another effort, she walked on, looking neither to right nor left because she seemed to be in an avenue of art shops and she wanted no more reminders of her lost love; no more reminders of Clive and his talent. But she had been so proud of that talent, so proud of his skill as a painter and scenic designer. It was hard to forget something that had mattered so much, or *someone* who had mattered so much.

She had to force herself to remember that he had gone out of her life and was never likely to come back into it. There could be no risk of that in Hong Kong.

And at that moment she saw his name, leaping at her in bold letters from an outsize poster.

Art Director: CLIVE FIELD

Diana stopped dead in her tracks. She was looking at an advertisement for the Elizabethan Shakespeare Company from London, in a repertoire of plays to be performed in the Lee Theatre of the City Hall as part of the forthcoming Hong Kong Arts Festival.

CHAPTER SIX

How long she stood rooted to the spot, she had no idea. She was aware of nothing but a wild excitement and a nameless dread. She longed to see him again, but feared it. To have

78

him walk back into her life when she had put so much distance between them was something she could not contemplate.

Fate couldn't do a thing like this, Diana thought wildly, but she went on staring at his name, which seemed to grow bigger and bigger the longer she looked at it. *Art Director: CLIVE FIELD.* Of course, he would naturally travel with the company. It was his job to supervise that side of every production. No stage manager could be responsible for supervision of that sort; only for erecting sets and dismantling them. Until she met Clive she had never realised just how much work an art director had to do during the run of a production, and certainly as big a company as the Elizabethan could not travel without one.

Automatically, her eyes scanned the names of the cast; all were familiar to her. Howard Butler, male lead, Godfrey Trease, second lead, and so on through the male members. And then the women. Gloria Dickson, leading lady, Phillida Brent, second female lead, Ethel Marchant, female character lead . . . She knew them all by name because Clive had talked about them a lot—especially, she recalled, Gloria Dickson. Dedicated, he had called her. 'She'll allow nothing and no one to stand in her way—that's why she's going to the top.'

To Diana, the woman's ruthless ambition had seemed implacable and hard. Not that it mattered, since they were never likely to

79

compete in any way.

Or had they been competing without her knowledge? Had Clive begun to cool towards her, Diana, from the time he had been engaged by the Elizabethan Shakespeare Company? It hadn't occurred to her at the time, but looking back now, she wondered. From that moment Gloria's name had cropped up more and more in his conversation.

She shivered, which was ridiculous because in this climate one was never really cold. Hong Kong was just within the tropics and the worst weather was the typhoon season, not yet due. This was a February evening, pleasantly warm with a certain amount of humidity which was always in the atmosphere of Hong Kong. And the Arts Festival was to open on February the twenty-sixth and last until March the twenty-fifth, which meant that Clive and the Elizabethan Shakespeare Company would arrive almost any moment now, in time to rehearse and prepare for their opening night.

*   *   *

On the third floor of the hospital, away from wards and theatre, was an office where the doctors and surgeons attended to all paperwork connected with their jobs. Next day, after Diana had finished her morning's reports, she went into the adjoining common room. Here, Medical and Surgical staff relaxed. Sometimes the atmosphere was a bit restrained by the presence of a visiting consultant—the interchange of specialists between the Government-run hospitals of the colony and the Kinsale was reciprocal—but today the only person present was Chris, who looked up with a cheerful smile and said, 'You're just in time. Coffee's just arrived and is piping hot.'

She drank some gratefully. After a sleepless night she needed a stimulant to keep her on her toes.

'Enjoy your outing yesterday?' he asked. 'What did you do?'

'Strolled round the shops and along by the harbour.'

'Not after dusk, I hope?'

'To tell the truth, I didn't notice.'

Nor had she. Stunned by that Arts Festival poster, she had walked blindly out of the Ocean Terminal and wandered aimlessly until hunger had driven her into a tea house packed with families playing mahjong at every table. Amidst the noise she had been as little aware of what she ate and drank as she had been of the crowds about her, except that, in contrast with herself, they had all been bubbling with enjoyment.

Chris noticed the tired note in her voice and the droop to her mouth. 'Are you finding it tough going, here at the Kinsale?' he asked sympathetically.

'No. The work presents no difficulties—'

'—but being the only woman doctor does? Is that what you mean?'

'No, again. All you men have been very co-operative.'

'Except one? I did warn you, remember. But I thought you must have won him over since he was so concerned about your having some free time yesterday. That impressed me no end, and you should take encouragement from it. Perhaps you're just homesick?'

She thought of the flat in London, directly beneath Clive's, and of the hours they had snatched together whenever Pearl was absent. She thought of her home in Somerset and her father's cluttered surgery, his packed waiting room, and the warm familiarity of the sprawling country house which had been her home until she became a medical student in London and answered Pearl's advertisement for a flatmate, and a swift nostalgia for the comfortable security of her childhood and girlhood descended on her.

How uncomplicated life had been in those days, with nothing to worry about except exams and fulfilling her father's ambitions! It had been his dream to have Diana working in partnership with him. He had taken it for granted that when she qualified she would do just that, but even so he had been very understanding when she announced her decision to take this job in Hong Kong. His kindly eyes had surveyed her with surprising perception as he said, 'Well, my dear, hospital practice anywhere will be valuable to you, and all doctors have to do a spell of it on qualifying. It will help you to get your M.D. all the quicker, which is important,' but, very wisely, he had refrained from pointing out that hospital experience could also be gained at home.

He knew about Clive, of course, and she had always presumed that her father liked him, though he had never actually said so. On parting, he had tried to let her know, in his understanding way, how much he felt her going. He had patted her hand clumsily, then kissed her on the forehead and said an unexpected thing—unexpected because he was not an articulate man about things other than medical.

'Remember this, my dear—wherever you go, you can't run away from love.'

How right he had been! She had brought her heart with her, with all its agony and frustration. She had brought the inescapable memory of Clive and now, ironically, he was following hard on her heels. Not even six-thousand-odd miles had been able to keep him out of her life.

She consoled herself with the thought that they were not likely to meet. A hardworking house physician, with little time off from the hospital, was not likely to mix in the strata of

Hong Kong society which drew visiting celebrities into their span. The worst she could anticipate was bumping into him on the street, and even that could be avoided by keeping away from the popular shopping areas and restaurants during the time of the Festival. Not that she could afford them, anyway. She would stick to the tea houses frequented by Chinese families, and when she had time to go swimming she would take a bus out to the New Territories and pick one of the unfrequented sandy beaches there. Theatrical folk would patronise only the fashionable spots, and remembering Clive's extrovert nature, Diana knew that any quiet little place, away from the public eye, wouldn't appeal to him.

Chris was saying something, and she jerked to attention.

'. . . we could do it together, if you'd care to.'

She stammered, 'I'm sorry—my thoughts were miles away—'

'So it seems! I was merely suggesting that we might see a few sights together, if we can arrange our off-duties at the same time. I'd like to show you around, and it isn't really ideal for a young woman to wander about alone in Hong Kong.'

'I'd love that—and thank you.'

The door opened and the R.S.O. entered.

'I saw your Mimi,' he announced. 'I took her to Hugo's at the Hyatt—damned expensive,

84

but worth it.'

'The devil you did! And how did you pull that off? I didn't tell you where we were meeting.'

'No need. I rang the French Consulate and asked for the Consul's personal secretary. When I got her, I apologised on your behalf and offered myself as a stand-in, which she accepted. I kissed her goodnight, moreover, and *how* she responded!'

'She's French,' returned Chris. 'She was thanking you for her supper. No more than that.'

'I suspect it could have been.'

With a sceptical wink at Diana, Chris departed.

'That young man should grow up,' said Maynard, pouring some coffee and drinking it at a gulp. He was due in the theatre in ten minutes.

'What was Mimi like?'

'True to type. I've met her counterpart in London and all over. Muldoon should look nearer home—he'd find attractive nurses under his nose if he troubled to notice them, and a damned sight less avaricious than private secretaries to French Consuls.'

And one nurse in particular, thought Diana, agreeing with him. The sooner Chris wakened up to Staff Nurse Chang, the better.

No sooner had the R.S.O. departed for the operating theatre, than the door opened again

85

and Jonathan Kinsale entered. Diana was surprised. Very rarely did the Super intrude into the medical common room, perhaps because he knew his presence would put a restraint on conversation. It never occurred to any of them that he himself would feel the restraint of an outsider, or that his elevated position at the hospital debarred him from this informal and enviable atmosphere.

He said, almost apologetically, 'I know the medicos have coffee here at this time of the morning. May I scrounge some?'

She was again surprised, for she had seen coffee being carried along to his office only a quarter of an hour ago, but she poured some at once.

'You don't look much better for your time off,' he commented. 'What did you do?'

'Walked, mostly.'

'That should have done you good.'

'It did.'

He looked at her doubtfully, and asked, 'Did you sleep last night?'

'Yes,' she lied.

'Not much, from the look of things. You have shadows beneath your eyes. I don't like them.'

She was startled. She would never have credited this man with having so much perception as far as she was concerned. Reading her thoughts, he added. 'It's the hospital I'm thinking of. Tired staff members are no use to me, or to the patients.'

To her own surprise she heard herself say, 'Would any woman doctor be of use to you, sir?'

'In the absence of someone better, she would have to be.'

She had asked for that, of course. She said, 'I'm sorry. I sounded impertinent. I didn't mean to be.'

He laughed. 'Oh yes, you did! You were annoyed and hit back in a characteristically feminine fashion.'

Diana felt the colour flame in her cheeks, and looked away. The next moment his hand was cupping her chin, turning her face to him. She saw his eyes looking down at her urgently, and his face drawing closer, then in one blinding, senseless moment their lips met, mouth clinging to mouth in passionate abandon. In his arms she was helpless, the strength of them pinioning her so that she could not move. Then suddenly, as if returning from insanity, he thrust her aside. She heard the door slam behind him.

*   *   *

Old Elisha's tired eyes surveyed the ward. A figure was coming towards his bed—a girl with vivid Titian hair, and wearing a white overall. She stopped beside him and the nurse who was about to feel his pulse stepped aside. The young woman nodded to her pleasantly and said, 'Thank you, Nurse—I shan't need you, but I see Sister at the end of the ward, looking very much as if *she* does!'

The nurse smiled and went away, and the young woman then put her fingers over his pulse and studied a fob watch pinned on her lapel. He saw a stethoscope trailing from her pocket and growled through his beard, 'Good lord, don't tell me you're a doctor! I'm damned if I'll be examined by any female!'

'So *you* are prejudiced against them, too! That's your bad luck, sir, not mine. And let me tell you that you were examined by me when you were admitted, though you don't remember anything about it, and you will continue to be examined by me so long as I am in charge of your case, which,' she finished politely, 'I *am*.'

She spoke briskly, but her voice and her eyes were kind. Nice eyes. Deep-set and wide apart. Not a conventionally pretty face, but striking. Interesting. He said, 'Turn to the light, will you? I'd like to examine *you*.' He chuckled. 'That surprised you, eh? You're obviously new around here, or you wouldn't be surprised by anything I say. Nobody else is.'

'So they humour you, do they?'

'Humour me, be damned! Why should I be humoured? I'm not an imbecile.'

'Just a pig-headed old man,' she agreed, smiling.

He shook with laughter. Even that left him exhausted. 'You've spirit,' he acknowledged, as soon as he had strength to speak again. 'I like a woman with spirit. Let me examine that face of yours again—I like it. When I'm out of this, I'll paint it.'

Even as he spoke, despair touched him. He knew well enough that he would never paint again. He had lost his touch years ago—or perhaps it was merely faith in himself. When a man didn't earn enough to buy canvases and materials, anxiety sapped his confidence.

He heard the young woman doctor say, 'I'll keep you to that.'

'To what?' he jerked, his tired mind groping back to the conversation.

'To your promise. I've never had my portrait painted. I might enjoy it.'

'More likely not,' he grunted. 'You'd find it boring and very tiring. I never had a model yet who didn't grumble, and swear I kept them sitting longer than I actually did.'

'I would time you! Though to sit still for long periods holds distinct appeal to a doctor who has tramped the wards all day, and attended Outpatients, and given a hand in Casualty, and been called out on Emergency. After that, any sit-down job is a rest cure.'

Old Elisha made no answer. His eyes wandered away into space again. My painting days are over, he thought hopelessly. I'll never handle a brush again, never touch a palette. It happens to artists sometimes, and it has happened to me. I'm finished. My talent is dead. Thank God, no one here knows who I am!

He felt the girl's hand on his wrist. His pulse was irregular and weak, his body emaciated. Diana said gently, 'Nurse is going to bring you some chicken broth and after that I want you to go to sleep. Promise you'll be good and do everything I ask? I understand that last time you visited us you discharged yourself before you were really fit to go. "Discharging yourself" is a polite way of putting it. I gather you walked out.'

'A man can't lie around accepting charity when he has to earn a living.'

'Nor can he earn it when he's unfit to work. I intend to build you up again so that you will work as never before, but I can't do it without your co-operation. You'll be put on a good nourishing diet, gradually at first, then building up to solids. When you're eating us out of house and home I'll discharge you, but not till then.' Her eyes sparkled with humour and kindness, so much so that he didn't like to argue. This idea that he could earn a living as a professional artist again was an illusion anyway.

As if reading his thoughts, she said firmly, 'I mean what I say, so mark it well! Once I get you fighting fit, there's no reason in the world why you shouldn't paint as you've never painted before.'

He muttered, 'I'm past it.'

'No one is past anything until they give in, and I am *not* going to let you do that. Here comes the chicken broth. Mind you down every drop!' She flashed her warm smile, and departed.

In her place stood Jonathan Kinsale. Old Elisha looked at him and nodded feebly.

'Knows her own mind, that one,' he commented.

Jonathan, who had been standing aside listening to the conversation, said, 'She was talking sense, you know.'

A nurse approached with a feeding cup. Old Elisha gave a weak croak of a laugh. 'Here comes my baby bottle! D'you think I'm in my second childhood, Nurse?'

*   *   *

Mae Wong was in her element when entertaining both Eastern and Western guests and seized on the slightest excuse to do so. The sudden arrival of her sister-in-law, Pearl, was as good an excuse as any other, particularly as she flew in at the same time as members of the Elizabethan Shakespeare Company, with one or two of whom she was apparently acquainted. The fact that Lee Wong was a prominent lawyer in Hong Kong and closely involved with the Festival

Committee also made it easy for his wife to throw a party for them, dignified by the term Reception, which had more appeal to Eastern minds and reflected Government House procedure.

Jonathan Kinsale had no doubt that tonight's event would be as successful as always, though he was not a party man himself. Beneath his reserve was a core of shyness which was chiefly responsible for his anti-social reputation. Nevertheless, he liked the Wongs and would never slight his hostess by refusing to attend, though he would have been far happier at home with his pipe and his books.

As medical superintendent he occupied a house in the grounds of the hospital—a doubtful blessing, he sometimes thought, because, being so close to his work, he rarely got away from it. Dedicated though he was, he sometimes felt the need for privacy, for a life of his own which could not be invaded, and for some inexplicable reason he had begun to hanker after this increasingly of late. Even more inexplicably, he had become aware of the solitariness of his life.

Because the night was clear and he felt the need for fresh air after a strenuous day in the theatre, he decided not to drive over to Hong Kong side via the harbour tunnel, but to take the ferry across. As he walked to the Star Terminal he found himself thinking of Diana

Freeman, reluctant as he was to recall that mad moment of passion between them. He preferred not to wonder what had prompted it, or what had made him take leave of his senses in such a way, but on one thing he was determined—it would never happen again. When they met, his attitude must be cold and professional. Not to meet her at all would be better, but in the course of work that would be impossible, so never must he give the slightest indication that he even remembered the moment.

He forced himself to think of her with professional detachment, acknowledging that as a doctor she seemed competent and that work didn't seem to frighten her, which surprised him. He had expected a girl of her age to be more interested in a social life, yet she had spent her first free evening taking a solitary stroll . . .

Of course, she might have friends in Kong Hong of whom he knew nothing, or she might have been accompanied by someone from the hospital; she hadn't actually said that she had spent her first free evening alone, and it was natural to assume that an attractive young woman would have no need to, but at any rate Chris Muldoon could not have been her partner because their duties had been switched. The thought was oddly consoling. It was also rather satisfying to reflect that he himself had been responsible for that.

Sailing across the harbour, Jonathan wondered why this girl occupied so much of his thoughts. He wasn't in love with her. How could he be, since he scarcely knew her?

Cars lined the road outside the Wong villa, and filled the courtyard too. Plainly the party was well under way, so perhaps he would be able to slip in unobtrusively and leave early. The Wongs' chief manservant received him with Eastern courtesy, and after greeting Mae and Lee, and being presented to Lee's sister Pearl, he made his way into the spacious reception room where everything was exactly as usual—the crowd, the mingled perfumes, the voices and laughter, the smoke, the chink of glasses. There was nothing to warn him that this evening was to be different from the rest.

He found a glass in his hand and, to get away from the crush, headed for a distant alcove—and came face to face with Diana. Her hair shone in the lamplight and she wore a dress which subtly emphasized the lines of her body. He wanted to retreat, but it was too late.

Mae Wong was circulating amongst her guests and at his side he heard her say, 'No introductions needed here! I will leave you two together—' She smiled and drifted away.

In their alcove, Jonathan and Diana were silent for a moment, then he noticed that her fingers were clenched tightly on the stem of her glass. So *she* was nervous, too. In a cool, confident, modern young woman this

94

surprised him. Surely it couldn't be due to any recollection of that passionate moment between them? She must have been made love to by many men. Young as she was, such incidents were just part of the business of growing up, accepted and forgotten.

But not by him. When a man reached his age he didn't give way to emotion lightly—not men such as he, at any rate.

But there was something touching about Diana's nervousness, her sudden shyness, so he gave her one of his rare, warm smiles and saw her eyes widen with relief. That quiet, withdrawn face of hers might very efficiently mask her feelings, but her eyes could never do that.

'I hope you are enjoying the party,' he said awkwardly.

'In a way. I enjoy looking on at all these people—they're terribly sophisticated, aren't they? Until I went to London I never went to parties much. Life in my home village was very quiet, and the parties I went to in London were never anything more than student affairs. I was hoping Pearl Wong wouldn't be monopolised by guests tonight—she was my flatmate in London.'

'So you have to accept me as a substitute companion. For a while, at any rate. I hope you don't find the idea too distasteful, particularly after our last meeting, for which I apologise.'

'I had forgotten it,' she answered negligently.

So it meant as little as that to her, as he had expected. He regretted even apologising, and to make conversation he said at random, 'Tell me about your home.'

'It's very ordinary. English and quiet. My father is a doctor and Mother died when I was small. After that, Father lived chiefly for his work.' She added hastily, 'That wasn't selfish of him. He adored my mother, so work was his salvation. She would have been happy to know that he found it that way.'

Jonathan had a sudden vision of a solitary child, the offspring of two people who had lived mainly for each other.

'So you went in for medicine because it was your father's wish. Did you ever think of going in for anything else?'

'Of course not.'

'Docile and dutiful,' he murmured.

A touch of colour flared in her cheeks.

'On the contrary, medicine always interested me, so your ridicule is unnecessary.'

'My dear girl, I'm not ridiculing. I am merely understanding you, perhaps for the first time.'

Before she could reply, a lull descended on the company and through a gap in the crowd Jonathan saw a tall, off-beat man enter the room, accompanying a woman whose face immediately attracted all eyes, and particularly

96

his own. Beneath his stunned surprise he heard a suppressed gasp from Diana, but only later did he recall it because right at this moment he was staring across the room at Gloria, the girl he had hoped and expected to marry.

CHAPTER SEVEN

He had never anticipated meeting her again because their parting had been final, their quarrel bitter and, he believed, beyond repair. 'When you come to your senses, Jon, you will quit that hospital in Hong Kong and offer your services to a good London hospital, and then we can both pursue our careers. You can't expect me to give up mine just to become a housewife in a narrow colony overseas! I would die of boredom. I'm an actress, and a good one, and my career is every bit as important as yours.'

It all came rushing back, the whirlwind courtship, the delirium, the shattering of the dream. They had fallen in love—or he had—almost at first sight. It had been a wild and deeply passionate affair, and he had taken it for granted that she would return with him when the remainder of his hospital furlough in London was over, but she soon made him realise that the idea of a wife going where her husband's work was centred was more than old-fashioned, it was selfish, but it didn't occur to her that gearing their married life solely to her career would be equally so. Their engagement had consequently been stormy, and they had clashed emotionally and temperamentally.

In retrospect, he realised that he had been possessive in his love; sometimes he blamed himself entirely for the break-up, but returning from that East End hospital, where he had been doing a year's specialist surgery, to an empty flat night after night, to find notes dropped through his letter box or, worse, a message on the Ansaphone, had been hard to take. It was a bleak homecoming. *'Darling, if you want to see me, you'll have to come along to the theatre—you can wait in my dressing room and after the show we'll go on to supper somewhere.'* Or: *'Don't ring me back, sweetheart. I'm doing a late spot tonight and you know you don't like hanging around until the early hours . . .'*

And when he had a merciful break from the hospital during the day, she would have rehearsals, or T.V. commercials, or guest appearances on panel games which were pre-recorded and which, later, they would have to sit up to watch if he were due back on duty very early in the morning, at a time when she wouldn't even dream of rising.

It had all been hopeless, a dismal forecast

for the future, and the disappointment of it had gone deep because Jonathan Kinsale was a man who felt things that way; he was emotional and passionate, capable of strong feelings, strong loves, and strong sentiments, and when people like that were hurt the pain was so great that they retreated, erecting a guard against further hurt. This was what he had done, determined to allow no woman to encroach upon his heart again.

She had piled abuse on his head when he announced his intention to return to Hong Kong at the end of his London stint. 'If you loved me, you would remain here!' she had stormed.

'If *you* loved *me*, you would come with me. I came here to widen my experience and to study new surgical techniques for a period of twelve months. Now the time is up, and I have to go back. The Kinsale is a family hospital, *my* family's. I wouldn't dream of working permanently anywhere else.'

'Nor would *I* dream of working anywhere else but London, so I'll wait here until you return. *I* am not slamming any door, so it is up to you to open it again.'

She was as confident as that, sure that he would be unable to live without her, but he had lived without her very well indeed and the hard shell in which he had encased himself had been a good protection against any possibility of falling in love again. He had even convinced himself that he was no longer capable of falling in love—until recently, and the reason for that he stubbornly refused to acknowledge.

Now he heard someone murmur excitedly, 'That's Gloria Dickson! She's here for the Festival—isn't she stunning? I wonder who the man is? Her fiancé perhaps? She's wearing a ring . . . Whoever he is, he's fascinating, I must say.'

And then his father's voice, at his elbow.

'That isn't *your* Gloria, is it, Jonathan?—the actress you were engaged to? I never met her, of course, but haven't forgotten her name. If it is, get your greeting in first—she hasn't seen you yet. Taking her by surprise will be good for both of you.'

Jonathan didn't ask why. He knew full well what his father was implying—that a sudden encounter would test not only her feelings, but his own, and both had to be faced. Even so, he hesitated, aware of a reluctance to meet her at all.

It was then that he recalled Diana Freeman's suppressed gasp and turned to look at her.

Like everyone else, she was staring at the newcomers, but particularly at the man, almost as if he too were a figure rising from the past.

And then Lee Wong's young sister Pearl was at her side, saying, 'I'm sorry, Diana, but how was I to know they would turn up here for the Festival? I swear to you that when I wrote to

100

Lee, I hadn't the faintest idea.'

'Of course you hadn't. How could you?'

Jonathan thought Pearl Wong looked faintly uncomfortable as she answered, 'Well, I could have predicted it, I suppose . . .'

'What do you mean?'

'Only that Clive did once ask me whether my brother had any influence with the Festival, but I didn't suspect that that was what he was after when he—when he—'

Diana looked at her friend for a long and discerning moment. She had forgotten all about Jonathan.

'When he started paying attention to you? Is that what you mean? Oh, Pearl, why didn't you *tell* me? Is he the off-beat man you've been seen around London with? I thought you helped me to get this job in Hong Kong for my own sake, not yours.'

'Well, I did partly, but not wholly, I admit,' said Pearl. 'So it serves me right, doesn't it? Being used by him, I mean. All he wanted from me was an introduction to the Festival Committee because he would like to be appointed its artistic director, a plummy once-a-year job in addition to his work in London. As far as his new love is concerned, it's been Gloria Dickson for ages, but neither you nor I realised it. Men like Clive aren't faithful to young women medical students or mere air stewardesses. He's the ambitious type.'

Briefly, Diana closed her eyes. She had to

get a grip on herself. Seeing Clive again was bad enough, but learning her friend's true reason for helping her get to Hong Kong was almost worse. What a naive, gullible fool I've been, she thought, but the realisation didn't lessen the pain one bit.

'Here—drink this. It will help.'

She opened her eyes, and saw Jonathan Kinsale holding out a glass to her. Pearl had gone, swallowed up by the crowd which now gravitated towards the glamorous actress and her companion.

Diana took the glass mechanically. It contained brandy and as the liquid fire braced her, she looked up at Jonathan. His eyes were quite expressionless, but some measure of his strength communicated and she was grateful for it.

'And now a breath of fresh air,' he said, and turned her towards the open french windows. She knew at once that he was offering her escape, and that she must have betrayed herself somehow. Had this disconcerting and disturbing surgeon guessed her secret?

It was at that precise moment that Clive saw her. A gap in the crowd was just large enough for him to catch sight of her head, highlighted by a glittering chandelier from above. For a second his eyes revealed no recognition at all; nothing more than a fleeting question, as if somewhere, sometime, he thought he had seen her before. Then his face stiffened in surprise.

That settled it. She wasn't going to run away.

She murmured, 'If you'll excuse me—I see an old friend—'

Jonathan let her go, but with mixed feelings. Rejection was most dominant, underlaid by anger and jealousy. He had heard every word of the conversation between Diana and Pearl Wong; in fact, he had listened without shame, and the Chinese girl's words echoed in his mind. *'It's been Gloria Dickson for ages . . . men like Clive aren't faithful to young women medical students . . .'*

So this was the reason for the secret unhappiness which his father had detected. Diana had come here on the rebound from a broken love affair, from a man who was apparently in love with his own ex-fiancée, and obviously that man was Gloria's escort. There was a bitter irony about the situation which made Jonathan Kinsale smile a little grimly. Neither he nor his junior house physician had suspected that tonight they were to come face to face with people who had been emotionally important in their lives—but the past tense apparently applied only to himself. It was plain that to Diana the man called Clive still mattered a great deal. That was why she drew away now, and waited for him to come to her.

From what Pearl Wong implied, the man had amused himself with both of them—though as far as Diana was concerned the flirtation had been only on his side. She must have been deeply in love with him to feel the need to put so much distance between them, and she must still be deeply in love with him to forget her pride as she was now doing.

He had an almost uncontrollable impulse to shake her, to tell her to come to her senses, then he shrugged and turned away. What did it matter to him? Why should he care? He had his own problems, but he was damned if he was going to run after Gloria or even wait to be noticed by her. It mattered little if she spoke to him or not. Nothing could be so dead as a dead love affair, so the jealousy which seethed in him couldn't be due to seeing her fêted and gushed over, with a man who was apparently her current lover. Or so he told himself. But the fact remained that her sudden re-entry into his life was a shock.

He tried to push his way to the door. Whatever advice his father cared to hand out, he intended to ignore. He was leaving this noisy party at once, and not only to escape Gloria. He refused to look on while his house physician made a fool of herself over that man, making no secret of her enslavement. If she wanted to be hurt again, let her *be* hurt, he thought angrily, and came to a halt against a barricade of guests, all straining to see the new arrivals. Celebrities were always lionized in Hong Kong society. He had seen it all before and would see it all again, only this time it was more irritating than usual.

'She's coming this way!' someone exclaimed. 'If we stay where we are, we're sure to be introduced.'

'It's the man whom *I* want to meet,' declared another; a woman, of course. 'He's the art director, the one who has been making a big name for himself in London—a fantastic designer, they say. Oh, bother! He isn't coming over here, he's going over there—'

And so he was—to Diana, waiting to meet him with her heart reflected in her eyes. Jonathan looked on bitterly. What a fool he had been to imagine that her heart had responded when he kissed her the other day, or that a passion which was not only physical had prompted her wild response!

And then Mae Wong was bringing Gloria across the room, introducing her to as many people as possible. Mae was a conscientious hostess who endeavoured to overlook no one, but inevitably the more pushing were the ones who claimed attention, and the group Jonathan found himself among were pushing indeed, so that against his will he came face to face with Gloria.

She was smiling, radiant, loving the adulation and the flattery, oozing charm as only she knew how, but the sudden sight of him caught her off guard. She was momentarily still, but only he was aware of it because her mechanical stage smile remained fixed on her face; she could hold it before spotlights and cameras for as long as required, a training which came to her aid at this moment. He was the only one to detect a hint of shock in her eyes, immediately covered with a dazzling assumption of delight.

'Jonathan, *darling*! How wonderful to see you!'

'Didn't you expect to? You knew I lived in Hong Kong.'

'But not that I should bump into you almost at once! We only flew in a short time ago—'

'Then you should be resting, otherwise jet-lag will hit you hard and you'll pay for it later.'

'Still the medical man, aren't you, darling? First, last and foremost the medical man . . .'

'Always,' he agreed.

Mae Wong was looking from one to the other, faintly puzzled. To Western ears their easy exchange revealed no undercurrents, but Eastern eyes, apparently inscrutable, were always capable of detecting the unseen.

'So you know each other?' she said lightly. 'That is one less introduction to make!'

'We know each other well. Very well, indeed. Don't we, Jonathan?' Gloria put a world of significance into her voice, and he knew what it implied. She was laying claim to him, reminding him of her prediction that he would never be free of her, that one day he would be ready and willing to reopen that door which she had refused to slam behind him. She hadn't changed one bit. These were tactics she had used in the past, usually after a quarrel, or when she wanted to remind him that he was her property, or even to proclaim it to the world. She would be doing that here in Hong Kong, if and when it suited her book.

He answered casually, 'We met a long time ago, but scarcely had time to get to know each other.'

'That can be put right easily, darling. I'm here for six whole weeks, including rehearsals, and I plan to stay on after the Festival. I thought a flat somewhere . . . a prolonged holiday . . . I need it.'

It was the first time the idea had entered her head, but now it seemed a good one. She had forgotten how handsome her ex-fiancé was; in fact, he seemed to have grown more distinguished. And what a contrast he was with theatrical folk! One could grow so tired of them . . .

'I am always very tied up at the hospital, but I am willing to meet for a chat somewhere,' Jonathan said levelly.

It was suddenly important to him to do so. He had to destroy, once and for all, any idea she might have that he could be picked up again at will. She must be made to see that he was no longer her slave, and that a man as passionate as he was capable of equally passionate rejection; and the sooner he made it absolutely clear, the better.

The friendly sparkle in Gloria's eyes now seemed to hold chips of ice.

'How nice of you, darling, but are you sure a man so busy can spare the time?'

'He could make it,' he answered dryly.

'You *will* make it—for me,' she murmured.

Both were now unaware of other people. Antagonism sparked them between them as of old, but neither his calm face nor her brightly smiling one revealed it.

Mae Wong intervened, drawing other guests forward to be introduced, and glancing around for her other celebrity. A stage designer didn't have the magnitude of a star, but this one had come to the party with Gloria Dickson and a rumour of their association had come ahead of them. To bring him into this conversation seemed a good idea; it would draw a little attention away from these two and give Jonathan Kinsale a chance to escape. With unerring instinct, his hostess knew he was wanting to do just that. She also sensed that despite this woman's beauty and charm, he saw what lay beneath the surface and didn't like it very much.

Mae didn't either. She preferred women like Diana Freeman, who didn't have one public face and one private. Where was she? It would be nice to bring her to the foreground. Unlike many guests, she didn't clamour to be noticed, or push herself forward to meet the guests of honour.

But there she was, talking to Clive Field already, and obviously unaware of anyone else. Mae went over to them.

'Come and meet Miss Dickson, Diana—and we can't have you monopolising our other guest celebrity!' She spoke lightly, but she meant it. Several women were waiting to meet Clive Field, whose success story had been written up in the *Hong Kong Standard* only this morning. But Mae had an additional motive for separating these two. Her young sister-in-law had admitted that Clive Field was the man she had been seen around London with, and that he occupied the flat above her own, and neither Mae nor Lee liked the idea of that very much. It wasn't only because, in their oriental eyes, it was undesirable for a young unmarried girl to live alone in a Western world, but because Clive Field displayed all the characteristics which offended their oriental tastes. Cosmopolitan and Western-integrated though they were, they still clung to the essential conventions of their race.

Apart from that, Mae felt that young Doctor Diana was too nice to be exposed to men like Clive Field. She didn't want either Diana or her sister-in-law to see too much of him. Let women like Gloria Dickson become involved, if they wished; such women could take care of themselves.

A moment later she was saying with impeccable Oriental courtesy, 'Miss Dickson, allow me to present Dr. Freeman—' and Gloria was smiling at Diana and saying in mock awe, 'A woman doctor! How clever you must be! I've never had that kind of a brain, have I, darling?'

She turned to Jonathan with a teasing, possessive smile, only to find that he was not looking at her, but at this young woman who didn't look anything like a doctor to her.

*   *   *

Diana was thankful for Mae's intervention. Meeting Clive had not been easy, although she hoped she had carried it off well enough. Her determination not to run away had been one thing, but to cling to it had been quite another. She had stood transfixed as he came towards her, unable to look away, held by the sight of his familiar, yet somehow unfamiliar, face and figure. In London his beard and his tousled hair and his rumpled clothes had seemed natural and endearing; now they seemed untidy and unkempt and somehow affected, the props of a *poseur* who was determined to be different, to be noticed, and more than all to advertise the fact that he was an artist and therefore unlike the rest of ordinary humanity.

'Well, Diana?' he greeted her, somewhat tritely. 'This is quite a surprise.'

'Isn't it?' She had forced a light note into her voice. 'I had no idea you were to be a guest too, though Pearl once told me that her sister-in-law entertains visiting celebrities and the Elizabethan Shakespeare Company is an obvious choice just now.'

Her glance had strayed across the room to Gloria Dickson, surrounded by admirers, among whom Jonathan Kinsale stood out. He seemed to be intent only on his conversation with her, and Diana felt bereft of an ally. But she had asked for it, hadn't she, turning away from him like that? In retrospect, her action appeared to be not only thoughtless, but ungrateful. He had helped her unobtrusively when Clive's arrival caught her off guard, and her sudden resolve not to run away should not have made her forget that.

For a moment she had wondered whether to follow him and explain, but the milling crowd had proved an effective barrier. The eagerness to meet 'glorious Gloria' had suddenly struck Diana as amusing; these people were like a pack of teenagers mobbing a pop star, she had thought, unaware that she smiled at the humour of it. Unaware, too, that Clive saw that smile and was surprised because it was uncharacteristic of the girl he remembered. Back in London, the attention of the adoring Diana had never wavered from himself.

'Isn't it amusing how people, whatever their nationality, always react the same way to the famous?' she said. 'I imagine Gloria Dickson would be fêted equally in London or New

York or Rome or anywhere else. She's lovely, Clive—even lovelier than on stage, and certainly lovelier than you told me.'

'Did I tell you?'

'Quite often.'

The light note was still in her voice. He took it to be indifference and he didn't like that very much.

He asked abruptly, 'What made you take a job in Hong Kong? There are hospitals in London.'

Diana wasn't going to admit that it was because of him, though somehow she felt it was the answer he wanted. Instead, she answered, 'I've always wanted to spread my wings, so I seized the chance.'

That surprised him, too. He would never have credited her with sufficient courage to break away from tradition, or to strike out for a life of her own.

'I always knew that London wasn't really your scene, but I pictured you going home and sharing your father's practice for ever.'

(And growing into an old maid in the process?)

She answered coolly, 'I wonder why.'

'It seemed the obvious thing for you.'

'But why should I do the obvious thing? I am not an obvious person, I hope?'

Apparently not. Apparently Clive had never really known her. When he first saw her this evening, he had almost failed to recognise her.

Her hair was different, for one thing. Back in England she had worn it tied in the nape of the neck; neat and tidy, with never a hair out of place. Now it hung to her shoulders, free and lovely, but the change in her was a great deal more subtle than that.

To his annoyance she made him feel vaguely uncomfortable—a unique experience in his life. He had made his mark in the theatre very rapidly, becoming something of a celebrity and having his pick of many women. Perhaps that was why the studious young medical student from the flat below had appealed to him; she was different from the rest. He had enjoyed bringing her out of her shell, enjoyed enslaving her, but once that was accomplished he had taken her for granted. Unlike Gloria. A man could never take a woman like that for granted.

Unable to feel at ease with this subtly different Diana, Clive had stared moodily in Gloria's direction, resenting the attention she was getting. He disliked being a woman's shadow, getting only a minor share of the limelight. Enamoured of her as he was, he begrudged her the lion's share of attention, though he was not surprised by it.

Apart from her acclaim as an actress, Gloria's looks alone merited attention. Taller than average, she held herself superbly and wore her striking black hair in a severe classical style—dead straight, parted in the

113

centre, and coiled in the nape of her long neck, like a ballerina's. Her features were beautiful, with high cheekbones, finely bridged nose, great dark eyes which she exploited to perfection, and a delicate but firm jawline. She was a natural for any stage or screen, and her beauty was made even more intent by her underlying sensuality. The most stilted of Shakespeare's female characters—Caesar's wife, Calpurnia—became a creature of flesh and fire when portrayed by Gloria.

By comparison, Diana had seemed almost a mouse of a thing, although he had always admired the vibrant colour of her hair. She had the pale skin of most redheads, and the amber-brown eyes that went with it, but she had never made the most of herself, never sought to be noticed. Now he glanced at her profile and saw the clear cut lines of it, the short straight nose, the full lower lip which seemed to balance her overlarge mouth, the deep-set eyes which had been free of make-up but tonight were subtly emphasized with silver-blue eye-shadow which seemed like a reflection of the unadorned silver-blue dress she wore.

She must have bought that in Hong Kong, Clive thought, for she never wore such clothes at home. Had he known that she had mortgaged a month's salary at Yengtoh's for this slip of a dress which looked nothing on a hanger but fabulous on a woman's body, he would have recognised Diana even less. She had never lashed out extravagantly on clothes at home, chiefly because she couldn't afford to, but something seemed to have got into her blood here in Hong Kong, and suddenly he visualised the woman she could become and saw her as the little nurse from Lotus Ward had seen her—as a girl any man would notice.

'Who is the man talking to Gloria?' he asked. 'Jonathan Kinsale,' answered Diana, 'medical superintendent of the hospital I belong to.'

'Your chief? No wonder you speak of him so admiringly.'

'Do I?'

'It's in your voice.'

'He's a wonderful surgeon.'

'Is that why you admire him?'

'Since I only know him professionally, it must be.'

(But that wasn't true. When a man kissed a girl the way Jonathan Kinsale had kissed her, she knew another side of him altogether . . .)

Conversation had petered out. In no way at all had this meeting with Clive resembled the reunion she had dreamed of. Glancing at the slim gold watch on her wrist, her father's twenty-first birthday present, nostalgia had touched her. She didn't really belong here, and her alienation seemed emphasized by Gloria Dickson's presence. She felt overshadowed by the actress's personality and wanted desperately to get away.

She had weathered the meeting with the man she loved; she had held her head up. If she could quietly escape . . .

At that precise moment Mae had drawn her into the circle, and after introducing her she continued, 'And now, Jonathan, I am going to pin you down for a theatre party—Diana also. We'll fix a date right away, so that I can be sure your hard-working house physician is off duty when the time comes.'

'You make me sound like a slave-driver, Mae.'

'From what I hear, you are! When can you both take an evening off together?'

Gloria commanded imperiously, 'It must be next Friday, when I play Rosalind! Don't you agree, Clive? You like my Rosalind best of all, don't you?'

Because her eyes were fixed on Jonathan Kinsale even though the words were addressed to himself, Clive snapped, 'No—Lady Macbeth. She's much more in character.'

The spark of anger in her eye pleased him. *Touché*, he thought. That serves you right for trying to torture me by pretending to be interested in this surgeon.

The man wasn't her type at all. Too quiet, too reserved, too serious. But any man was food for Gloria's vanity. Why I put up with it, I don't know, Clive reflected sullenly. She's always doing this—flirting with some man or other in front of me, just to flaunt her appeal and to emphasize her independence. That's the devil of it. If I take offence, there'll be a dozen men to take my place, and well she knows it.

The party had gone stale on him. It had started off well enough, with Gloria the centre of attention and himself at her side, envied and admired. He had been very sure of himself when they entered the room, quite unprepared for the meeting with Diana. Somehow things had seemed to go wrong from that very moment. He had even felt that she was indifferent to him, though he refused to believe it. Diana couldn't have got over him so quickly, so she must have been putting on an act.

He heard her saying brightly, 'Friday would be lovely! It's my day off, so I won't have to do any duty switching.'

Clive frowned. Gloria saw it and was pleased, taking it as a sign of jealousy. She liked it very much when he was jealous. She was always careful not to let Clive become too sure of himself, so it was good for him to realise that she was above him. She guessed now that he frowned because Jonathan was coming to see her perform. There could be no other reason.

But when Diana left the party, with nothing more than a friendly wave in his direction, Clive watched her departure with a feeling of personal affront and even a touch of regret. Devotion from another woman could be a desirable thing when Gloria flaunted her own indifference and set him aflame with jealousy. Diana had never been exciting in the way Gloria was exciting, but she had been loyal. He had believed she would continue to be, but now he wasn't so sure. That casual wave of farewell left him with the unfamiliar feeling of being no longer the victor, but the vanquished.

CHAPTER EIGHT

Outside the air was cool. Diana lifted her face to the sky and saw a million stars scattered there, like sequins on a billowing skirt. Even Hong Kong seemed quiet, although it was a place that never slept.

From the tall windows of the Wongs' villa, light spilled into the courtyard and the street beyond, revealing the lines of waiting cars and Diana's shadow etched sharply on the pavement; a slim shadow, silver-blue in the moonlight, walking alone. It seemed solitary and a little lost.

To her surprise, tears spilled on her cheeks and because she was alone she didn't bother to wipe them away.

Below, the brilliant harbour lights seemed to flood a strange and alien world. What am I *doing* here? she wondered. And what good did it do me, coming so far from home? She was a girl who had run away from love, only to find that she couldn't escape it.

The night air was comforting and she decided to walk from the Mid-Levels down to the Star Ferry. After the performance she had just put up she felt in need of solitude, but not ready for the loneliness of her room. Had she only had an escort, she could have turned into any bar or club or place of amusement, visited the Poor Man's Market which flourished only after dark, to the Chinese Opera or for supper on a floating restaurant in the sampan village of Aberdeen, where hundreds of families lived their entire lifetime on the water in a vast huddle of vessels. But she was alone and had to be content with a solitary walk and her own thoughts.

She prayed that no one had seen through her bright pretence tonight. Least of all Clive. How great had been her effort to appear casual and at ease, only she would ever know. Now reaction was setting in and she was powerless to fight it.

Footsteps echoed behind her, but she paid no heed until they reached her side and a voice said, 'We can pick up a taxi outside the Hilton. Meanwhile, I suggest you dry your eyes and forget about that man—at any rate, for the present. Doctors have little sympathy for patients who give way to self-pity, but that is

119

precisely what you are doing at this moment.'

It was Jonathan Kinsale, of course. No other man would have been so brutal or direct. He never pulled his punches—which, at the moment, was a good thing. Diana rallied defensively and said, 'Thank you, I prefer to walk.'

'Ridiculous. You can't walk to Kowloon, unless you're prepared to trudge all the way to Wanchai—not the most salubrious place at any time, day or night—and then take your life in your hands through the traffic tunnel where, I'd remind you, pedestrians are forbidden anyway. And if and when you reached Kowloon side, you would still have the long walk to Haiphong Road and the hospital. Those flimsy shoes wouldn't stand up to a trek like that, so we'll take a walla-walla instead of the ferry, then only I will see your tears.'

She choked, 'I'm not crying!'

'Then for heaven's sake do so, and get it over. After that, we can talk.'

'There's nothing to talk about.'

'Oh yes there is. I want to know why a doctor on my staff should be emotionally entangled to such a degree that the sight of a man walking into a crowded room can upset her. What do you do when examining a patient? You list their symptoms, analyse, prescribe and, I hope, finally cure. *Physician*,' he quoted, *'heal thyself.'*

120

She hated him for being so unfeeling, and yet was grateful. It made everything easier to deal with. She sighed, and the sound touched his heart, though he took care not to show it. This was not the moment to sympathise, though he could easily have done so. He had gone through a somewhat traumatic meeting himself tonight, and only hoped he had hidden it well. Reserve was his armour, and he had worn it for so long that nothing could persuade him to discard it now. Without armour, he was as vulnerable as the next person.

He said briskly, 'That man was important to you. Quite apart from the fact it was obvious, to me at any rate, I admit I heard every word Pearl Wong said, and I don't apologise for listening. Now I want the whole story.'

'It concerns no one but myself,' she answered shortly.

'On the contrary, it concerns me very much. Staff problems must be settled for the good of the hospital. We must decide how to deal with yours.'

Of course—the hospital would always be his first consideration.

'I'm sorry,' she said, and he answered a little gruffly, 'Don't be. Talk instead. Bottling things up won't help, and it's always easier to talk to strangers because they are not involved.'

'*Strangers may kiss and pass by . . .*' She had heard that quotation somewhere, and was surprised to hear herself utter it.

'They not only may, but do. It happens all the time.' The indifferent note in his voice was surprisingly hurtful. So it had indeed meant nothing to him, that passionate moment which she would never forget and which, she realised now, had lingered in her memory. She had thought less about Clive since it happened, and but for his unexpected re-entry into her life, she might well have ceased to think about him altogether in time. Now she was almost glad he had come to Hong Kong, reminding her of the past and their romance. Perhaps it had been more ardent on her side than on his, but there had been a shared ecstasy which had lasted for more than a passing moment. In that, he had been more genuine than this man.

Her lips tightened angrily. She resented Jonathan Kinsale's assumption that she could be kissed furtively and then discarded. The thought blinded her to the fact that there had been nothing furtive about it, that he had not locked the door like some sly philanderer in melodrama, and that he had totally disregarded the fact that any doctor or surgeon could have walked in and found them together in a thoroughly compromising situation.

'All right,' he said now, 'if *you* won't talk about it, I will. You love him—'

'We loved each other,' she corrected.

'But it didn't last. Love affairs often don't but, like measles and other childish complaints, they have to be lived through.'

'What do *you* know about love?' she cried. 'To you, it's merely biological!'

Her words echoed in the silence, and the darkness hid his bitter smile. His engagement to Gloria, brief as it was, had been a great deal more than merely biological—on his side, at least. He had cherished romantic dreams about living happily ever after and raising a family.

They crossed the square in front of City Hall, where rickshaw men lined up by day and left their empty rickshaws stacked in neat rows by night, and reached the waterfront. Walla-wallas rocked at the foot of some stone steps in the harbour wall. He handed her into one, took his place beside her, and the vessel headed for Kowloon side, the waterman's face turned away from them. But there was no need for such discretion. Diana sat as far away from Jonathan as possible which, in such a small space, had its limitations. Aware of her nearness, he could not resist slipping an arm around her shoulders and drawing her close.

His desire for her was intensified; stronger, in fact, that it had been the other day. He had to exercise the sternest self-control.

As far as Diana Freeman was concerned, he was serious. The realisation came as a shock. *This* was the reason for his sudden determination to be free of Gloria once and for all. He was no longer content to drift on in the same old way, living only for work. That dream of a real marriage stirred again.

He saw her young profile etched against the lights of Kowloon, which were reflected in a path of gold across the water. They were sailing right into it, like a cockleshell searching for the foot of the rainbow. Oh, *my darling,* he thought helplessly, *if you only could love me as you love Clive Field! I would carry you off to the end of the world and cherish you forever.*

Five minutes brought them to Kowloon side, and as the walla-walla came to a halt Diana said anxiously, 'I only hope Clive didn't guess how I felt.'

So that was all that mattered. Clive's feelings, Clive's reactions. His own counted for nothing. Why should they? Jonathan thought bitterly. I've done nothing to endear myself to her from the moment of her arrival.

He answered, 'I shouldn't worry. You gave an excellent performance.' His voice was totally impersonal, and after helping her up the harbour steps he dropped her hand as if he had scarcely been aware of holding it.

They walked back to the hospital in silence. Side by side they mounted the front steps. He would see her safely inside and then return to his solitary house in the grounds. His man would have left the usual tray of drinks and laid out his night clothes, and the whole place would be as immaculate and without soul as any bachelor establishment.

He had furnished it with taste and character, and liked it well enough, but now he had no desire to return to an empty shell, comfortable as it was.

The wide stone wall of the hospital greeted them, with broad stone stairs rising from the centre. More stairs went down to kitchens and offices, and prominently displayed facing the main doors, was a large portrait of the Kinsale who founded the place. Jonathan never entered without a feeling of pride, a feeling of homecoming. It had an atmosphere peculiar to no other hospital, a personal touch which endeared it to almost everyone. He saw a reflection of his pride in Diana's face as she paused and looked around, and his heart quickened.

'Do you feel it already, Diana?'

She nodded, knowing what he meant. 'What is it about this hospital that gets you?' she answered.

He looked at her for a long moment. Her face was pale, but there was no longer any trace of tears. Her cyes were lovely, her mouth sweet and softly modelled. He felt himself being drawn towards her once again, but resisted.

He said gently, 'Then there is room in your heart for something more than Clive Field. My dear, you are on the road to recovery already.'

She smiled. For a man who lacked a heart he was extraordinarily perceptive and uncannily right. There was room for no other man but Clive in her life, but there was room for this hospital, a place dedicated to the relief of suffering. The Kinsale could be her refuge and salvation.

There came a sound from above, the sharp echo of footsteps running down the stone stairs. It was Staff Nurse Chang and her face was taut with anxiety.

'Mr. Kinsale—sir—can you come, please? Quickly! It's old Elisha—there's been an accident!'

*   *   *

Elisha lay very still. His face was grey, streaked with ugly gashes which showed up like rivers marked in red upon a map. He breathed irregularly and lay at a distorted angle.

'He'd been restless all evening,' Dorothy Chang said, 'declaring he was well enough to be discharged and that he'd had enough of charity. You know the way he goes on, sir—'

Jonathan nodded. His skilled eyes and hands were already taking stock of the man's condition. 'Tell me precisely what happened and what has been done.'

'He wanted to reach the fire escape, the one leading from the men's ward, but the door leading to it is kept locked. When I left the ward for a minute he managed to climb up to a window. The fire escape runs down outside it, and he fell on to the iron steps. That was how his face was gashed—on the edge of the treads. We took him to X-Ray. Sister will tell you—'

The radiologist, hurrying into the ward at that moment, took up the story.

'Three fractured ribs—one penetrating the lung.' She held out the wet films; Jonathan held them to the light and read them with a practised eye.

'Where is the surgeon on duty? Who is on duty, by the way?'

Sister said tartly, 'Mr. Muldoon, sir—or supposed to be.'

Dorothy Chang interrupted swiftly. 'He was called out on an emergency, sir.'

'And the R.S.O. ?'

'Tonight he's off duty. I tried to get him, but he was out for the evening.'

Jonathan said reasonably, 'He is entitled to be. What about this emergency Muldoon went to? Where did the call come from?'

Dorothy Chang hesitated, and Diana guessed she was hiding something. Was she covering up for Chris, and, if so, why? That young man was conscientious about his work, so why the necessity to shield him?

Dorothy began nervously, 'I—I don't know, sir—but I could find out.'

Diana didn't believe that. The girl was playing for time. Something had gone wrong. She saw the anxiety in Dorothy's eyes give way to relief as Jonathan said, 'Never mind. We've an emergency right here on our hands. I'll start work myself and perhaps Muldoon will be back in time to lend a hand. Has Theatre been alerted?'

'I telephoned through as soon as I saw the X-rays.' The radiologist's voice was a trifle smug. 'They're already standing by.'

Diana cut in, 'Can't I help?'

Jonathan answered, not ungratefully, 'Muldoon is House Surgeon, so it's his job to assist. I expect he'll be back in time.'

He left the ward and walked towards the theatre. All but Sister followed. As Jonathan entered the changing room, Diana caught Dorothy's arm and held her back.

'Where is he?' she whispered.

'Oh, Doctor, I don't know!'

'Tell me the truth.'

'Well, he—he didn't report for duty. He's been absent all evening.'

Diana stared.

'I don't believe it! Chris may be irresponsible outside the hospital, but he'd never let the firm down.'

Dorothy said miserably, 'That's what I thought, Doctor, but he hadn't arrived by the time the R.S.O. went off. Mr. Maynard wasn't worried. He said Chris would be sure to turn up, but I felt uneasy because he has always been punctual. It just isn't like him!'

'Go and find him. Take a taxi. I'm sure you

know his haunts.'

From beyond the door, Jonathan Kinsale called, 'Doctor Freeman—do you think you can really help?'

Diana went towards the changing room. Her party dress looked incongruous in the bare space. She said, 'Of course, sir,' but when he looked her up and down uncertainly she added, 'I studied surgery as well as medicine, in the usual way.'

She couldn't resist that. She saw a flicker of amusement lighten his stern eyes, then disappear.

'Be as quick as you can, please.'

He went into the theatre and she into the female changing room. She stepped out of the silver-blue dress and it fell in a gossamer pool on the floor. A nurse put out a theatre dress and apron and found her some shoes. She then picked up the blue dress and carried it away. Diana knotted her smooth hair and covered it with a surgical cap, then walked to the scrubbing-up trough where she removed her nail varnish and scrubbed thoroughly. The nurse dexterously held out a sterile mask, then a gown and tied its voluminous folds securely around her slim figure. Then Diana held out her dripping arms and the nurse asked mechanically, 'Wet or dry, Doctor?'

'Wet, please.'

The girl poured sterilised glycerine on to her hands and she pulled on the gloves.

A few steps and she was at Jonathan's side.

Beneath the shadowless lights the table waited and, a moment later, the trolley appeared, carrying old Elisha's inert form. Was it really only yesterday that he had said to her, as the sound of wheels passed the ward door, 'They'll never trundle *me* on the agony-wagon, Doctor! I may be worn out, but I'm not broken . . .'

But now he was. Badly.

He was placed on the operating table and the anaesthetist went to work. Only the sound of the old man's breathing—uneven, stertorous—filled the lofty room. Diana saw Jonathan Kinsale's eyes above his surgical mask. They were dark and intent, but beneath that intensity was such compassion that her heart was moved.

Which was the real man—the cold stranger whom she normally saw, the surgeon looking down at his patient with concern, or the man who had kissed her with such passion that her senses reeled?

Soon the anaesthetist announced, 'Ready now.'

Jonathan began to work. It was the first time Diana had seen him operate and the skill and dexterity of his fingers impressed her. The superintendent of the Kinsale Hospital knew just what had to be done and, lifting the shattered bone, he proceeded to repair the lung, working at top speed whilst the

130

anaesthetist kept an eye on the patient's respiration and pulse rate. Elisha was old. He was undernourished and tired. An accident in his condition could prove fatal, so speed with precision was essential. A surgeon needed an able assistant on such an occasion, and to his relief he found it in Diana Freeman. Later, when he was alone, he admitted to himself that no man could have served him better.

He dealt with the chest himself, and then, as if he felt his deputy assistant deserved some reward, he left the facial stitching to Diana, watching critically as she sutured the wounds. She came through with flying colours.

When everything was over and Elisha had been wheeled back to the ward, Jonathan disappeared into the changing room, where he shed his theatre garments and a nurse thrust them into a linen-bin. Back in the theatre, Diana felt acutely disappointed. He had uttered no word of thanks, no word of praise or even encouragement.

Like an automaton she walked into the female changing room, where she peeled off her rubber gloves and untied her gown. It fell from her like a loose tent. A nurse took it and made some joke about it and Diana smiled mechanically. She reached up and pulled off her surgical cap and her hair fell in a cloud about her shoulders. She looked very young, the nurse thought, standing there in bra and pants, with loosened hair: tired, too.

The girl smiled and ventured to remark, 'Parties take their toll, don't they, Doctor?'

Diana nodded. It was hard to believe that this was still the night of the Wongs' party. So many things had happened. Meeting Clive again, betraying her secret to Jonathan Kinsale, facing up to his censure, and finally helping in an emergency op. Events had placed an emotional strain on her and now she wanted nothing so much as to drop into bed and turn her face to the pillow. In the absence of comfort from another human being, it was her only refuge.

It seemed absurd to step into a party dress after a session at the operating table. Theatre staff glanced at her as she left, but she was quite unaware of their admiration. Sister's Theatre comment meant more to her. 'Well done, Doctor,' the woman said, and Diana stepped into the corridor with a lighter heart.

To her surprise, Jonathan was waiting.

'I'm taking you out to supper. Party nibbles aren't exactly sustaining—we've both earned something more substantial. Gaddi's, I think—'

At that very moment, Staff Nurse Chang emerged from the male Residents' Wing with Chris Muldoon.

*   *   *

Dorothy Chang was feeling both triumphant and apprehensive, and with good reason. She

132

felt even worse when meeting the Super. To come face to face like this was something she had not anticipated. All she had prayed, since finding Chris sprawled on his bed, was that the operating session would continue long enough to get him on his feet and in some shape to report for duty, but he was obviously running a high temperature and not fit for work.

She had raced down to Pharmacy, begging for a speedy remedy to bring down a patient's fever and brushing aside the dispenser's demand for written authority. 'Sister told me to ask you to act at once—I promise to bring you a signed chit within the next hour!' (Time enough to worry about that, time enough to explain to a disapproving Sister . . .)

And time enough to worry, later, about breaching hospital rules, one of which was that no member of the female staff visited the men's rooms, but where else could she look for him when every other possibility proved fruitless? Nor had she really expected to find him there, since telephoning had brought no reply. Knocking on the door had been a last resource, and what instinct had made her open it when no response came, she had no idea. But a good thing she had, for there he was, cheeks flushed, forehead hot, pulse racing. Professionally, she had a clinical thermometer in her pocket and put it immediately into his mouth. As she expected, his temperature was high.

But at least she had managed to get him on his feet, half coaxing him, half bullying him, scolding him for not having so much as an aspirin in the place. 'You look after other people, why can't you look after yourself?'

'Don't bully me,' he had said thickly. 'Do you realise what I've done? I've let the hospital down. I'll be sacked—and deserve to be.'

She had grasped his hands then, unaware that her own were trembling.

'It isn't too late! That stuff from Pharmacy works fast and I'll help you downstairs. If we hurry, you can at least put in an appearance, and you won't have to explain or apologise—anyone can see that you're ill!'

'Anyone?' he had echoed as she dragged him to the door. 'What d'you mean—anyone?'

She told him what had happened and he rallied with a jerk. 'The Super? That's torn it! I'm finished, Lotus Blossom. The fact that I didn't even send a message before the R.S.O. went off, will damn me in Kinsale's eyes.'

'But you couldn't help it. You can explain.'

'All the explanations in the world won't excuse the fact that I failed to report for duty.'

'But the Super doesn't know you didn't report. I said you'd been called out to an emergency. Don't look at me like that, I had to say *something*! Maynard had gone off and I couldn't think of any other way to protect you.'

To her astonishment, he rounded on her. 'D'you think I want your protection? What sort of a creep d'you take me for? If I have to take a rap I'll take it without hiding behind a nurse's apron.'

It was then that they reached the main hall and came face to face with the Super. Jonathan looked at him hard, and then at the diminutive figure of Staff Nurse Chang. 'So you fetched Mr. Muldoon from his 'emergency', Nurse?'

Diana saw the girl's anxious little face, and pitied her. Just how deeply she loved Chris Muldoon was obvious. If he left the hospital the bottom would fall out of her world.

Chris said, 'There was no emergency, sir. Nurse just assumed so, when I didn't report for duty.'

For a moment Jonathan's features remained stern, then he took another long hard look and said, 'You're swaying on your feet, man. You're not fit to be out of your bed. Why the devil didn't you send a message through to theatre, saying you were ill? Nurse, have a side ward prepared; it's no use Mr. Muldoon taking to his own bed for the next forty-eight hours. He can be more conveniently nursed nearer the wards. And ask Sister to take a look at him herself. Since the R.S.O. cannot be contacted, I've asked the consultant physician to stand in and Sister Theatre has made a note of Gaddi's number so that I can be called there, should there be another emergency.' Then his voice softened. 'And who said you didn't report for duty, anyway? What are you doing now, I'd like to know? Well, get along—don't just stand there. Dr. Freeman—I hear our taxi.'

His hand was beneath Diana's elbow, sweeping her to the door and down the steps outside. Chris Muldoon and Dorothy Chang were alone. She took hold of his arm, turning toward the stairs, taking charge with brisk efficiency, but he pulled away.

'Next time I want you to fight my battles, Nurse, I'll call on you!'

Hating himself, dizzy and angry and ill, he stumbled up the stairs.

CHAPTER NINE

The night was well advanced by the time Jonathan and Diana left Gaddi's. In silent consent they walked back up Nathan Road and along Haiphong to the hospital. The street was deserted and it seemed the most natural thing in the world for his arm to link with hers and for their footsteps to slow to a leisurely pace. Such a starlit night was not meant for haste; it was meant for love. She was most potently aware of him and had to sternly resist an impulse to draw closer to his side, but the touch of arm against arm and the movement of their bodies, in rhythmic step, charged his blood, so that suddenly and without warning he gathered her close, kissing her hair, her eyes, her cheekbones, her throat, murmuring her name incoherently until his lips settled upon hers and clung there passionately. Time and place seemed to fall away, leaving them suspended in ecstasy, the deserted street forgotten; the whole world forgotten in the wild passion of their kisses.

She felt his strong body trembling, and her own responded, desire and longing clamouring to be satisfied.

'Oh, my love, my dearest love,' he murmured, and she knew that his longing was as wild as her own, his desire as great. Then his mouth was devouring hers again and his arms were crushing her body against his, so that they seemed to merge into one. She never wanted to be free.

It was he who broke the enchantment, suddenly coming to his senses and thrusting her aside. 'I'm sorry—' he said abruptly, 'I'm sorry—' and, taking her arm, he walked on without another word.

Before parting at the main entrance of the hospital he said, 'Forget what happened just now. I lost my head . . .'

But not your heart, Diana wanted to say, and found herself incapable of speech. Those wild moments of passion had affected her profoundly, but she was determined not to let him know. She heard herself murmuring stilted thanks for the evening, ignoring the culmination of it, and she heard him say in return, 'Take tomorrow off. You've earned a rest.'

'But with Chris off too—'

'We'll manage. I'll do double duty myself.'

She wanted to thank him, but feeling that appreciation would embarrass this unpredictable man, and still feeling shaken after those breathless moments in his arms (had they *really* happened?) she found herself incapable of saying anything more, except to murmur a trite goodnight. And so they parted, both vitally aware of each other and both afraid of showing it.

Preparing for bed, Diana pondered on the enigma of this man; stern and remote one moment, passionate and tender the next, but always making her strongly aware of him, whatever his mood. She remembered how he had turned his back on her in the operating theatre, uttering not a word of thanks for the help she had given. She hadn't done her work badly, either; in fact, when working with him she had felt inspired. And then there had been the incident with Chris Muldoon, when he had noticed the young man swaying on his feet and had thawed into humanity again. At a moment when she had expected him to flay that young man alive, his heart had revealed itself.

And it had revealed itself even more as they walked down an empty street, beneath a starlit sky, and his reserve had vanished beneath an overriding passion, only to be followed by an abrupt rejection. What sort of a man was he—brilliant, moody, unexpectedly humane, physically passionate, tender, ruthless, caustic and even cruel? Did these things make up the sum total of Jonathan Kinsale's character, or were there secret depths which he kept hidden?

In the dark, unable to sleep, she was haunted by his face. If she had been a sculptress she would have liked to chisel his features out of granite—but that was cold and unyielding; a hard and ruthless material. It could never soften as Jonathan's face had softened when he looked at an unconscious old man on the operating table.

The thought of Elisha brought his bearded face floating into her consciousness and again, tugging at some stray cord in her mind, came that feeling that it was somehow familiar. Sometime, somewhere, she had seen this man's face before—but where, and when?

Suddenly she resolved to find out. If only to prove herself wrong, she had to establish old Elisha's identity. She had to discover more about him.

*   *   *

Sister Casualty was surprised when Doctor Diana arrived early next morning, asking to see the Outpatients register. At a hospital the size of the Kinsale, Outpatients and Casualty had to be housed in one department, with Sister Casualty in charge of both. She was too busy to enquire why the house physician wanted to see the register, which was lucky because Diana wanted no one to suspect what she was up to.

Old Elisha appeared to have had a number of addresses in the course of the past few years. Occasional admissions were marked 'No Fixed Abode', but on his recent arrival he had given an address in Wanchai—No. 9, Lei Street. Diana made a note of it and set off immediately.

She boarded a trolley car on Central Street, ignoring the stares of its passengers, who were exclusively Chinese and, in the main, ill clad. Passengers for the Wanchai district were inevitably poor, standing in the open space at the rear where one could travel for as little as a cent. For three cents she was privileged to take a seat inside, where she sat alone, watching with alarm as non-paying passengers hung on to the outside of the vehicle, swaying perilously as it speeded along the tracks with barely enough space, between passing trolley cars, to accommodate a human body. At such breathless moments they flattened themselves against the battered metal sides, emerging miraculously unscathed.

Although she was aware that Wanchai was a notorious district, nothing had prepared Diana for the full impact of its narrow, squalid streets, its swarming humanity, its garish clubs which were blatantly vice dens, its noise, its ceaseless jangling music, its filthy alleys and pavements, its young inhabitants with old faces and old faces which looked as if they had never been young. And more besides. Inscrutable eyes which seemed to follow her, padding footsteps which seemed to echo in her wake— but when she looked round, everyone seemed to be unaware of her and intent only on going about their business, or staring vacantly into space.

The streets grew narrower and became cobbled, without any form of sidewalk and with barely enough room to pass between market stalls and the mean houses which seemed to pitch drunkenly at angles, propping each other up—doors without hinges, windows without panes, doss houses for squatters, sleeping places for the homeless. Neither sun nor happiness could ever penetrate here.

Apprehension seemed to crawl up Diana's spine like a living, chilling creature. To go either forward or backward seemed to promise nothing but a trap. All she could do was press on, looking neither to right or left. The hopelessness of her quest now thrust at her. To find Lei Street in this sprawling maze, where street names were either missing or were too begrimed to be readable, was obviously going to prove impossible.

She tried to memorise the map which she had studied as she crossed on the ferry. It had seemed quite straight-forward, Lei Street being off Ladder Street which, she knew, was one of the most famous streets in Hong Kong—on a par with Cat Street and Lascar Row in the Central area, the den of thieves and vagrants. She groped in her handbag for the map, but common sense urged her not to stand still to study it; she was conspicuous enough as it was, the only Western woman to be seen, and walking alone. She tried to keep on the move. There must be an end to these teeming streets. Even Wanchai had its boundaries.

Clutching her bag under one arm, she unfolded the map and tried to read it as she walked, but now it made no sense at all. Without knowing her exact bearings, it was useless. She thrust it back, dodged a passing cart laden with what looked like refuse but was a load of rotten vegetables being plied for sale, and found herself in yet another street of flimsy market stalls selling dubious fish, skinny chicken legs, and unidentifiable dried creatures which looked like nothing so much as dead vermin.

The stench was sickening. This was an aspect of Hong Kong she had never expected to see, a hideous contrast with its beauty and elegance. Deformed beggars held out clawing hands; bundles of rags on broken pavements suddenly stirred; girls with painted oriental faces waited by windows, half stripped, with some wrinkled crone taking payment at the door. Men sat in groups at rickety tables, smoking long clay pipes, and women of all ages queued beside a kind of barber's chair, waiting their turn to submit to what was considered by the Chinese to be the most beautifying process of all—the the removal of every trace of down from their faces and the shaving of the hairline back from their brows so that they could present to the world a high smooth forehead and unblemished skins.

Without thought, Diana stood still and watched. The process was done with a long waxed thread pulled taut and then rolled repeatedly across the contours of the face, then dipped in soapy water and manipulated again. The woman barber was old and bent, but her skill was undeniable and it was obvious that her customers felt no pain—and that however poor they were, essentials of life would be sacrificed for this ritual.

Suddenly aware that she, in turn, was becoming the focus of attention, she crossed the alley quickly and, turning out of it, saw a street of pitching steps rising high before her. Ladder Street—it had to be! It matched the pictures she had seen of this famous thoroughfare. And off it was Lei Street, where old Elisha lodged.

Excited, she almost ran up the first flight of

stone steps, then forced herself to proceed more slowly. She had counted the turnings on the map—Lei would be the third from the top and was therefore quite a way to go, for Ladder Street climbed up towards the sky, where trees were silhouetted. Up there Wanchai ended and respectability began with middle class houses and shops. That, of course, was the way she should have come, had she only known how to get there, but at least it would be her way back.

At last she reached the third turning from the top, as narrow and dubious as the rest, but with its street name still clinging to the decaying wall, and just readable.

Lei Street. Number Nine. She had to count the houses one by one, ignoring the watchful stares of occupants at windows and squatters on the pavement. Mercifully, the figure was displayed on a peeling door which stood open to the street, as the door to all Wanchai houses seemed to be.

She took a breath and stepped across the threshold. To her surprise, a woman emerged from the shadows—white-skinned, brassy blonde and coarse in a way which characterised only Western women. Even the pathetic Suzy Wongs of the district displayed the inscrutable dignity of the oriental, however harsh their lives, as if some inner core of refinement remained immune to sordid reality. But the owner, if owner she were, of No. 9, Lei

Street, advertised her past way of life.

To Diana's surprise, she spoke with a genuine Cockney accent. 'Wotcha want, love?'

How could she ask for Elisha's room? The woman wouldn't know him by that name, so she asked if an elderly English gentleman lodged here. 'An artist, white haired and bearded.'

'Y'mean old gaffer Jones? Not that that's 'is reel name, I'll bet, but I arsks no questions of me lodgers unless they don't pay their rent, which, I might add, 'e 'asn't done for the parst month, which is prob'bly why 'e's done a bunk.'

'He is in hospital. The Kinsale. I have come from there to collect some things for him.'

'No go, ducks. I 'old wot me lodgers leave, in loo of rent. The old fool left the key in the door and I'm keepin' it. 'E ought 'ave known I 'ad another, anyway.'

'No doubt he left it there because he intended to return. He collapsed and was admitted to the Kinsale. Tell me how much he owes, and I'll pay it.'

The woman named a sum which Diana didn't believe, but which she just managed to meet, with some small change left over for the return journey to Kowloon side. Then she held out her hand. 'The key, please.'

It was handed over without another word.

'And the room?'

The brassy head jerked and the cigarette dangling from a corner of the mouth spilled ash down a dirty blouse.

'Top floor back.'

It was easy to find. The bare wooden stairs terminated on a small landing with a door to a front room and one to the back.

Diana had never seen so pathetic a place. There was a bed or sorts, a rickety table and chair, a cracked wash-basin, and a cheap wardrobe which stood agape, revealing a few threadbare clothes. Oddly, the pathos of the old place lay in its cleanliness, a sharp contrast with the narrow hall and stairs. Recent dust on the sparse furniture was the only indication that its owner had not been around to deal with it. The floor was bare—the window too. Beside the window stood an ancient easel and on it was a half-finished canvas—a painting which troubled Diana because in its whirl of colour was confusion and despair and fear.

She touched the meagre collection of dried-up paints, the almost worn-out brushes. Were these pitiable materials all the old man had to work with? If he was too poor to buy paints, no wonder he had given up hope.

She turned away, and light from the begrimed window focused on the opposite wall, pin-pointing something which made her heart stop.

It was a picture, and although she had never seen it before she recognised Clive's work. Drawing nearer, she saw his signature, immature and less flamboyant than it was now, but undeniably his.

There were others—all unframed. Oils and water colours, pastels and pencil sketches, all specimens of Clive's work which the old man had obviously treasured through the years.

With a shock, she guessed his identity, though search the room as she might she knew she would find no proof of it.

She took down the pictures, wrapping them inadequately in a piece of tattered newspaper. Let the harridan downstairs enter this room with that other key, if she wished—she would find nothing valuable to steal now. No doubt she had regarded these unframed paintings as worthless daubs, otherwise she would surely have sold them. That was one bit of luck, at least.

To disguise the contents of her parcel, she wrapped a few clothes in more tattered newspaper and carried both parcels together as she descended to the murky hall, where, as she expected, Madame awaited, hand extended for the key.

'The room is mine,' Diana told her. 'I paid the arrears of rent and more besides, so you are not entitled to this key any more. And the rent will continue to be paid until further notice. And if I find that anyone has been in there and helped themselves to anything, there'll be trouble.'

The woman sniffed and called after Diana's retreating back, 'Nothin' worth touchin', anyway!'

She was out in Lei Street again, wondering how a Cockney woman came to be running a lodging house in Wanchai, and giving a shrewd guess. An ex-cabaret dancer, no doubt, who had remained in Hong Kong and drifted into more profitable business until age took its toll. A piece of Western flotsam lacking the dignity and honesty of the elderly lodger in the top room back.

CHAPTER TEN

As expected, Gloria's Rosalind was a triumph and Mae's theatre party a huge success. Afterwards they all gathered in Gloria's dressing room to toast her in champagne. She received their praise as if it were rightful homage, and radiated a charm which embraced everyone. Particularly the men. And, Diana noticed, particularly Jonathan.

Although he had escorted Diana to the theatre she had seen little of him throughout the evening, and when they all went on to Hammond Kinsale's penthouse later she saw even less, because he made no effort to resist Gloria. It even seemed that he sought her company deliberately. That should have pleased Diana, because it released Clive, whom she particularly wished to talk to, but in that she was also disappointed. At a crowded party it was impossible to have a private conversation with anyone, though Jonathan and Gloria seemed to be succeeding well enough. When two people wanted each other's company they could always contrive it; in her case, it was only she who wanted Clive's and this he seemed studiously to avoid.

As always, he was in his element at a party and tonight he was getting his lion's share of attention. His sets for *As You Like It* won everyone's praise and justified his increasing reputation as a scenic designer. Perhaps he knew that from Diana he could expect appreciation but not fulsomeness, so she had to wait her turn for a word with him.

Meanwhile, her glance kept straying to Jonathan and Gloria, whose conversation appeared to be wholly absorbing.

Beside her, a voice said, 'I haven't had a chance to welcome my favourite lady doctor—' and there was Jonathan's father, smiling down at her. 'I've been hearing great things of you. Not that they surprised me. And now, if you're truly feminine, which I can tell you are, you'll be wanting to know what I've heard, but hesitating to ask. Well, you have a right to know. My son has been praising the work you did the other night, on Elisha.'

'He hasn't said a word to me!' Diana exclaimed.

'My dear, did you expect him to? Not

Jonathan. When you know him better you will value his silences as much as his utterances. There is a certain worth in that, you know. And now I see you're observing the deep conversation going on between him and Gloria Dickson. Do you mind?'

She was startled. This old man was too observant. 'I wasn't aware of them,' she lied. 'My thoughts were miles away.'

How many miles? he wondered. I'd say no more than ten yards, and that those yards stretched merely as far as my son. And that pleases me. But how would this girl react were I to tell her that I too would like to know what the pair of them are talking about so earnestly? Even more important, how would she react were I to tell her that once upon a time he was going to marry the woman he appears to be so absorbed in?

But that would be cruel to both her and Jonathan, two people whom he had no desire to hurt. Not for the first time, Hammond wished his son's engagement could be broken off as finally as the closing chapter of a book, but from the determined expression on Gloria's face he suspected that for some reason or another she was more intent on starting it all over again.

He was right. At that very moment, Gloria was saying 'Darling, I don't agree with a word you say. Of *course* everything isn't over between us. All right, we've not seen each other for a long time, but there's nothing to prevent us from coming together again.'

'Except that I don't want to.'

'So you said long ago, and had my answer.'

'Still being dog-in-the-manger?' he enquired.

'Not a bit. That proverbial creature wouldn't let any other creature have what he didn't want or couldn't get, but I do want you, darling, and as your fiancée I am entitled to have you.'

'My ex-fiancée,' he corrected.

She shrugged that aside. 'I know I was silly and perhaps a bit selfish, but I've learned my lesson.'

'How?' he taunted. 'Who taught you?'

'No one. Just life. Life in the theatre, the toughest life in the world.'

'Don't tell me you're tired of it.'

'But that is just what I *am* telling you. I have had the success I sought—'

'So surely you want to hang on to it?'

Gloria shook her head sadly. 'I thought you would understand, I really did. How old was I when we fell in love?'

'Three years younger than myself, which meant you were old enough to understand the responsibilities of marriage, and old enough to take them on. But you didn't. Or wouldn't. Anyway, what is the use of raking over dead ashes?'

'None—if they really are dead, which I don't

believe.' Her lovely eyes became pleading. 'Jonathan, I beg you, give me another chance.'

'For what?' he asked brutally. 'To terminate things if and when you feel inclined?'

'That would never happen, I promise. Seeing Hong Kong has opened my eyes. I had no idea it would be like this.'

Her glance encompassed his father's beautiful home, the luxury, the roof garden with its panoramic view of harbour and mountains and distant islands scattered on the South China Seas. 'And what a climate, after England!'

'You would hate it when the typhoons came,' reminded Jonathan.

She dismissed that. 'Typhoons don't last all the year round.' (And surely they could get away quickly when typhoon warnings came? One could fly to every corner of the globe from Kai Tak).

'While they're raging, you think they're going to last for ever. Have you visited the hurricane shelters for the sampan people? You should. And then imagine hundreds of them, huddled together for days on end down there.'

'Darling, don't be absurd—we wouldn't be living on a sampan. We'd be snug in our own home.'

'Not mine, Gloria. Can't you accept the inevitable? Can't I get through to you? Can't you, or won't you, grasp what I'm trying to say? I want to hold on to my freedom because it's important to me.'

'You've had your freedom all this time.'

'Not freedom to marry,' he said steadily.

For the first time, she was too surprised to answer.

'Why the astonishment?' he asked. 'Didn't you expect me to fall in love with someone else? Well, I admit *I* didn't expect to, either, but it has happened, and by God I don't mean to lose her.'

And by God, I'll see that you do, she fumed inwardly. 'Who is she, Jonathan?' she demanded.

'No one you know.'

'But someone I've met?'

Jonathan made no answer. He wasn't going to reveal his secret to anyone. Besides, he didn't trust Gloria one bit. He didn't trust her revived interest in him, her desire to be reunited, or any of her promises. Nor did he trust her not to be vengeful, a capacity she had revealed in the past.

'You have Clive Field,' he said bluntly. 'Isn't he enough for you?'

'Frankly, no. I'm bored with him. I was never in love with him, anyway.'

'But you had an affair with him, even so. Perhaps it's still on?'

She gave her tinkling stage laugh. It carried right across the room to where Diana and his father were seated, and it sounded like a laugh of pure happiness. Hammond heard it too, but to his experienced ears it sounded ominous and determined. Something had to be done about this woman.

He heard Diana murmur, 'Excuse me—I want to have a word with someone.'

Hammond rose as she moved away, and remained standing as he watched her cross to Clive Field, now within convenient reach. He heard her say, 'Clive—I must talk to you. It's important', and at that identical moment his son, who had at last wrenched himself free from Gloria, wended his way toward them. What Diana said next, as she seized Field's arm and held on to it, Hammond missed, but Jonathan didn't.

'Please, Clive—I *must* see you! Alone. I've been trying to get hold of you all evening.'

He shrugged. 'O.K., so you've got hold of me now, but d'you mind not hanging on quite so desperately? People will imagine things.'

No need to imagine them, Jonathan thought. That impassioned note in her voice and the pleading in her eyes spoke for themselves. Was she so desperately in love with this man that she had no pride?

He turned away, but their voices followed him. She was insisting that she must talk to him privately, and Clive was giving in.

'All right, no time like the present. What's it all about?'

'It is too personal to discuss here. Too important. People might overhear and I don't want that. Meet me somewhere soon—there's a tea house called The Sickle Moon opposite the hospital, and I'm off duty for an hour tomorrow between afternoon and evening surgeries—'

Clive hesitated, but Jonathan didn't wait to hear more. He went over and joined his father. Hammond allowed a touch of reproof to enter his voice as he said, 'You haven't wasted much time in getting together with that woman you were going to marry.'

And all for nothing, Jonathan thought grimly. Even if a miracle occurred and Gloria ceased to be tenacious, he couldn't delude himself that he had any chance with Diana. Despite his straight talk the other night, she was still enamoured of Clive Field, so what hope in heaven was there for him?

He turned his back on her as he said to his father, 'I haven't "got together" with Gloria, but she wants to get together again with me.'

'And you're particularly anxious not to, despite the fact that there is no other woman in your life. This seems significant. In what way, I wonder . . .'

'As you said to me a short time ago, let me live my own life in my own fashion.'

'And you quoted it back at me in defence of your decision to continue with a frigid, isolated existence. I take it you don't want to any more.'

Jonathan nodded, but said no more. He

didn't need to. Unbeknown to him, his wise old father had guessed the reason.

*   *   *

Clive agreed to meet Diana at the tea house at five o' clock the next day, and with that she had to be content. Throughout a busy morning she wished she had taken a chance right there and then to tell him about Elisha, but a doctor didn't reveal a patient's secrets in front of people, particularly patients who mattered a lot.

She was pleased to find the old man faintly truculent when she visited him. It was a good sign.

'I feel like a trussed chicken! For goodness' sake, Doctor Diana, get me out of this straightjacket!'

'That plaster stays on until you're ready to come out of it. Fractured ribs take time to set.' Her voice was brisk, but not unsympathetic.

'Especially old ribs like mine, eh? I'm a damned old nuisance, aren't I?'

'Not to us.'

'Not even when I fall out of windows late at night?'

'Only if you intend to make a habit of it. You're the one who has to bear the consequences, don't forget.'

He chuckled.

'I like you, Doctor Diana. You don't bleat a

lot of insincere platitudes. You bully a bit, but I'd rather be bullied by you than pampered by anyone else.'

'You *are* being nice this morning,' she smiled.

'A change, isn't it? I know what some of the nurses around here call me. Old Sour-Puss.'

'They mean it affectionately. As a matter of fact, we all like you quite a bit. Surprised?'

'Very. Why should you like a cantankerous, poverty-stricken old scrounger like me?'

'Cantankerous? Sometimes. Poverty-stricken? Lots of people call themselves that when they merely can't pay their income tax. A scrounger? I don't agree. The Kinsale is here to look after people who are sick, so you qualify. So you're not a scrounger. All the same—' She hesitated, then plunged. 'I would like to know a little more about you.'

The ward was quiet. At her desk at the far end of the long room a staff nurse was busy, her trim head bent over her notes. Through the glass door panel Diana saw Dorothy Chang's petite figure go hurrying towards the women's ward. She hadn't seen her to talk to since Elisha's accident, but in the fleeting glimpses she had caught, the girl appeared to be pale and unusually quiet, her bright vivacity gone.

That puzzled Diana. If she was in love with Chris Muldoon, as she undoubtedly was, surely the fact that he had escaped dismissal should have made her happy?

Diana's fleeting inattention was curtailed by Elisha saying, 'What would you like to know about me?'

He would have told anyone else to mind their own business, but to this girl he couldn't say it.

'Anything you like to tell me.'

'And if I don't care to?'

'Then you don't, and I won't pry.'

He hesitated.

'You want to know who I am.'

'But you can't remember, can you?'

Again a hesitation.

'No. I can't.'

She touched his hand. 'Lots of people have tried to lose their identities.'

'Meaning that I'm trying to lose mine?'

'Meaning that you're trying to hide it, though I can't think why.'

Elisha's eyes looked very tired; his voice was also tired as he said, 'Let say I'm a penniless artist and leave it at that, shall we?'

'I was once in love with an artist,' she said slowly.

'Was? Meaning you're not now?'

'Meaning just that.'

'If he let you go, he was a fool.'

You wouldn't say that if you knew who he was, she thought. You wouldn't treasure his pictures, even when you're starving, unless you thought highly of him. She wondered how the old man would feel if he knew that those pictures were now stored in her room.

She asked, 'Why were you so anxious to leave the hospital that night?'

He hedged. 'I've been here too long. I didn't expect to stay more than a day or two.'

'You were very weak. If you hadn't been so weak you wouldn't have swayed and fallen from that window. Why try to leave before you were discharged, whole and well again?'

'I was anxious about something.' He looked at her thoughtfully, then made up his mind. 'I can talk to you, Doctor Diana. You're not one of those bossy nurses who think they're only here to order a patient about.'

'That's not fair,' she reproved. 'All nurses aren't bossy, and those who appear to be may simply be over-worked and pressed for time. *I shouldn't be lingering here now. I was due on* Women's Medical five minutes ago and if the Super should come along, he won't be pleased.'

'Why is everyone around here afraid of him? Why stand in awe of him? He's a man, like any other.'

Oh no—not like *any* other, she thought.

'You say you can talk to me—then do so. What do you want to tell me? Your reason for anxiety? Was it about someone?'

'No. I have no relatives, thank God. I was anxious about things I possess. I'd left my door unlocked and these things are in my room. I don't suppose any of the tenants would miss me, or bother to go into my room if they did, but there's a harridan of a landlady who's no respecter of anyone's property and if she thought I'd skipped without paying my rent, she would seize everything. Even my dried-up paints could fetch a cent or two. But the pictures are worth far more, especially to me. So I wanted to get back there—'

'Would you like me to collect them?'

'It's too unsavoury a place for a young woman to visit alone, but maybe you know of some man who would go? I'd be grateful.'

His voice shook, and Diana said gently, 'Don't worry, I'll see to it.'

The ward door opened, admitting Jonathan Kinsale.

He surveyed the room for a moment, then came across. 'I'll give you the address,' Elisha was saying. 'No need. I can get it from Casualty.'

She patted his hand and turned to go, and came face to face with the Super.

'I've just visited Women's Medical, Doctor. The Sister told me you haven't yet done your morning's round there.'

Elisha piped, 'My fault—I hindered the lass.' Diana smiled at him sweetly.

'Our conversation was no hindrance at all. I appreciated it.' Then to Jonathan: 'I'm going immediately, sir.'

The words were dutiful, but the tone was

not. It challenged him to punish her, which he very much wanted to do.

CHAPTER ELEVEN

Clive was surprised to find that Diana was not waiting for him at the tea house. He had fully expected her to be, not merely because the hospital was across the road, but because her eagerness to see him indicated that she was still in love with him, despite the impression he had received, at Mae Wong's party, that she had changed in a subtle way. How absurd to think that she ever would!

So naturally he expected her to be the first to arrive for their date, as in the old days.

The din of Mahjong from every table, coupled with the shrill, incomprehensible chatter of Chinese voices, began to grate on his nerves as he waited. For two pins I'll get up and go, he thought angrily, then decided to be generous and wait another five minutes.

It was ten before she appeared, and he was still there, but not for the world would he admit that he had arrived on time.

'Sorry I'm late, Clive.'

'Are you late? I've only this minute arrived myself.'

'Good. Waiting for people to turn up can be infuriating, can't it? But I was held up on the wards, then I had to dash upstairs to my room to get this.' She indicated a package wrapped in old newspaper. His glance amused her. 'Don't turn up your nose—this was the only available paper and I haven't had time to lay my hands on anything better.'

She took a seat opposite him, dropping her yellow linen coat over the back of her chair. The plain white dress beneath, designed to fit snugly beneath her white medical overall, was simple and effective. She had good lines to her body; long and well proportioned. Clive was suddenly remembering them well . . .

He ordered tea, then said. 'You picked a helluva place for a private chat. In this din, we can hardly hear ourselves speak.'

'It would be the same anywhere at this hour. You'll get used to it.' She seemed amused by his irritation. 'Mahjong must be the noisiest game in the world, and not surprisingly—there are a hundred and forty-four tiles to a set and four players to rattle them.'

'Tiles?'

'Those pieces they play with.' Diana glanced at her watch. 'I haven't much time, so let's get down to it, shall we?'

She seemed to be calling the tune, and he didn't quite like it. 'Get down to what? You make it sound as if we have something specific to discuss.'

'So we have. These.' She opened the package. 'It must be a long time since you

162

painted these, Clive. They are your work, aren't they? I knew as soon as I saw them, and of course they bear your signature.'

He stared. 'Where in the name of heaven did you get these? Good grief, I must have done them years ago! They're undeveloped, raw, immature—'

'But full of latent talent, and very precious to the man who taught you.'

Clive's head jerked up. '*Matthew Wade?* Do you know him?'

'I think so.'

He demanded eagerly, 'Where did you meet him?' Boredom and petulance had vanished. 'You can't think how much I'd like to see the old boy again. I owe him a lot—'

'Everything, you once said. That is why I took these.'

'Took them?'

'From his room, a day or two ago.'

'*Here in Hong Kong?* For God's sake, give me his address! I tried to contact him once, but no luck. Then I heard he'd taken off somewhere, but hadn't an idea where.'

'And it didn't occur to you that it might be Hong Kong, even though you must have known that he loved the place? You once told me that he talked about it a lot. The East was his passion, you said, hence your appreciation of Eastern art. So when he "took off somewhere" you could surely have put two and two together.'

'What are you hinting?' Clive said testily.

'That you couldn't have looked for him very hard.' He resented that note of censure. 'I wrote to the last address I had. He didn't answer.'

'So you left it at that?' queried Diana.

'Why not? If he'd wanted to keep in touch, he would have done so. Besides—'

'Besides, you were so busy being successful that you had no time to wonder if other people were being *un*successful.'

The tea came. She gathered up the pictures and rewrapped them. Then she poured the fragrant China tea.

'Matthew Wade discovered you, didn't he? I remember you telling me how he found you as a boy, obscure and likely to remain so. You told me once that your parents left you without a penny, that you were taken care of by distant relatives who sent you to a children's home when they emigrated to Canada. He found you in that home, didn't he? Didn't he come there looking for a child as a subject for a painting, and choose you?'

Clive admitted it unwillingly. It was so long since he had recalled the past that the memory of it came to him with a sense of shock.

'I've never made any secret of my background,' he muttered defensively. 'I've always acknowledged my debt to Wade.'

'But never paid it.'

'Look here!' he protested. 'I justified his

164

belief in me. I was a good pupil. Wasn't that enough?'

'At the time, perhaps, but not now. He's ill, right across the road at the Kinsale.'

'Poor old devil! I'll come along and see him. Bring him some grapes or something. When are visiting hours?'

Diana's eyes blazed.

'How wonderful of you! How generous too, especially towards a man who virtually adopted you! Not only that, he bought you your first paints and brushes, recognised your talent and fostered it, made you the success you are. You owe him more than a bunch of grapes!'

He stared in astonishment. He had always known her as a quiet, equable girl who idolized but never criticised.

He flung back, 'What right have *you* to judge?'

'The right of a doctor who cares about her patients, and the right of a human being towards another human being. There's something you don't know about Matthew Wade, something you could have found out if you'd taken the trouble to search for him thoroughly. Something you could have prevented, what's more. He's not only ill, he's destitute.'

After a moment, he answered slowly, 'I don't believe it. I don't believe a word of it.'

'All right. Come with me to his hovel off

Ladder Street and see for yourself. See the squalor of his surroundings and his meagre possessions—a handful of dried-up paints, a worn-out palette, brushes no artist could work with. Don't ask me how he came to such a pass—you're an artist, so you should know that sometimes tragedies occur when tastes and fashions change in art. He's one of the old school, I imagine, and the old school hasn't had much of a look in lately, has it? And a man with a generous heart doesn't save much for a rainy day. And I can guess why he never answered your letter—pride wouldn't let him. He wouldn't want you to know what was happening to him. He's so proud that he even conceals his name from us at the hospital.'

'Then how did you discover it?'

'I guessed, but not until I saw your pictures, pinned pathetically on the walls of his wretched room. His face was vaguely familiar, but I couldn't place it. I knew I hadn't met him before, but felt convinced I had seen his face somewhere. You once showed me pictures of yourself as a boy, taken by him and with him. You had press cuttings about him, too.'

'I still have them.'

'I'm glad,' Diana said quietly. 'He was younger then, and now he's old and ill health has changed his face a lot, but the shreds of his former self are there. And of course only one person could have possessed your pictures.'

'Not necessarily. Someone could have

166

bought them. I was selling my work as long ago as that.'

'And would an unknown buyer have refused to part with them even when starving?'

Clive shook his head unwillingly, and the silence lengthened between them. He was even unaware of the rattle of Mahjong tiles. Finally he asked, 'When can I see him? This evening?'

'You really want to?'

'Of course I want to! What sort of a man d'you take me for? All right, I've been thoughtless and selfish, but I can make up for it, can't I?'

His anger pleased her, but she asked just how he intended to make up for everything before she would agree to his visit.

'In every possible way, of course. You say he has some miserable room—'

'Squalid, and in Wanchai, of all places. Have you seen Wanchai yet? Wait until you do!'

'Then I'll get him out of it, house him decently, put him on his feet again.'

'You'll have to do it carefully, with subtlety,' she warned. 'The slightest hint of charity, and he'll take himself off again.'

'All right, all right—I'll go about it the right way, I promise. So when can I see him?'

'Tomorrow would be better than this evening, and I'll tell you why. When you come, I want you to bring these pictures with you. I want you to tell him that *you* took them from his room. Say we went together if you like, though I know he wouldn't fancy the idea of my going into the depths of Wanchai—'

'Then I'll tell him I went alone, that you gave me his address—'

'—which I got from the Casualty records, which is true. He has been worried about losing these pictures, afraid they might be stolen from his room. He even asked if I could arrange for someone to collect them—a man, because the Ladder Street area isn't an area for a woman to visit alone.'

'But *you* did,' he said, surprised.

'I didn't know how bad it was, and when I found out—well, I was glad I'd been. But I couldn't let him know I had gone there secretly—it might have seemed like spying. He can be very touchy, poor dear. Asking me to fix things was different, and naturally I thought of you. Now you understand why I couldn't tell you in front of all those people last night, don't you?'

He understood a great deal more. That he had deluded himself about the urgency of her desire to see him, that he had been vain enough to believe she was still in love with him. She wasn't. Something had indeed happened to Diana here in Hong Kong. Her job, perhaps? Certainly she had more poise and confidence, but he felt a secret regret for the loss of the girl whose devotion he had taken for granted.

168

He said almost humbly—real humility would never come to Clive—'I'm grateful to you, but I need hardly say that. I'll show you instead. I'll look after him until he's on his feet again, I promise.'

'And that you'll never lose touch with him again?'

'That, too.'

Diana handed the package across, then slipped into her coat. 'Bring them in this tatty newspaper—he'll know then that they were wrapped on the spot, and nothing could convince him more than that, that you did so yourself. And thank you for not disappointing me. Thank you for turning out to be what I believed you to be.'

He smiled, but it was rueful and not a little self-deprecating. 'I never deserved that halo you pinned on me, and I'm not sure I want it, either.'

She laughed. 'Haloes don't fit human beings, anyway.'

They said goodbye outside The Sickle Moon. Clive stooped and kissed her, and she let him.

'That's for old times' sake,' he said, his hands still on her shoulders, drawing her close again. 'And this is for today and perhaps the future.'

He kissed her again, and across the road, from a window of his house in the grounds of the Kinsale Hospital, Jonathan looked out and saw them. He turned away sharply. She hadn't wasted much time in picking up the threads of her love affair, he fumed, and beneath his anger was a hurt which went deeper than he cared to admit.

So he didn't see Diana draw away from Clive, shaking her head in refusal.

'Not for the future, Clive—that belongs only to me.'

And to someone else, she prayed, knowing her prayer to be futile.

*   *   *

Dorothy Chang was on duty when Clive called next day. He came into the ward with a line of visitors, pausing on the threshold to scan the row of beds.

'Can I help you, sir? You've called to see someone?'

He was on the point of asking for Matthew Wade when he remembered Diana's warning not to reveal the old man's identity to the hospital staff. 'We must respect his secret,' she said. 'A man who has once been famous, and then sunk into obscurity, can be sensitive.'

So he said to the pretty oriental nurse, 'Elisha, please,' but before she had time to speak he saw the old man lying, apparently asleep, in a distant bed, changed but still recognisable. He forgot the pretty little nurse at once. He was unaware of her start of surprise, because the sight of his old tutor had stunned him.

He walked slowly down the ward. Sickness and deprivation had left their mark on Matthew Wade's face, and although Diana had warned him of this, Clive had been unprepared for the reality.

The old man's eyes were closed, so he was unaware of Clive's figure halting at the foot of his bed. But Dorothy Chang wasn't. Her curious glance followed the visitor down the room. She was wondering how it came about that an unknown man should ask for Elisha by the name invented by the hospital staff.

Matthew Wade was not asleep. Nor need he have been in bed. He was perfectly mobile in his plaster cast and could have walked about the ward, had he wished, but he was saving that until all visitors had gone. At this hour, when friends and relatives visited other patients, his own loneliness seemed emphasized, so it was his custom to feign either indifference or sleep. He found pity galling and because this was frequently displayed by fellow patients and their visitors, he dodged it by pretending to take an afternoon nap.

Of course he insisted to himself that he didn't want visitors fussing about his bed, but now, lying with his eyes closed, he wondered how long it would be before he could leave the hospital and retire into obscurity again. In that room in Wanchai he at least had privacy, untroubled by anyone except occasional encounters with that aging trollop of a landlady, whom he knew how to deal with effectively. But when he went back there, how would he recover from a setback like this? At one time he had been able to supplement his diminishing resources by conducting English-speaking tourists round Hong Kong, but since ill-health had dogged him, even that had been denied him.

Memory was taunting him this afternoon. Since revealing to Doctor Diana his anxiety about his pictures, he had intensified it in his own mind. If that bitch of a woman had stolen them, he would have nothing left to treasure; nothing to remind him of happier days or the boy whom he had come to regard almost as a son.

Self-pity was not in Elisha's nature, but now he was too sick at heart to fight depression. He was tired of struggling, almost tired of hoping, but because he knew that if hope died the heart died also, he held on to the belief that a tide must always turn.

He didn't profess to be a religious man, but his way of life had been based on Christian beliefs and now, as always, words from the Bible sustained him. *For the Lord will not cast off for ever . . . yet will He have compassion according to the multitude of His mercies . . . they are new every morning . . .*

172

If people read the Bible as regularly as they read newspapers, they would worry less and fear less. That was his belief. Faith was what the world needed, but the world sought it in the wrong places, in the wrong ways. *Charity suffereth long and is kind . . .* simply meant love. Charity was a much-abused word. There had been nothing smacking of charity, in the accepted sense, in the way he had loved that boy, whom he regarded as his own child. He believed in him then and he believed in him now. One day he would come back into his life. It was simply that work had taken possession of him. When a man was carving a career for himself he had to devote all his time and energy to the job. And no doubt the boy believed him to be as comfortable as ever, which was what Matthew wanted him to believe.

All the same, it would be like the answer to a prayer if he were to open his eyes now and see him standing there, with that slightly arrogant but endearing smile on his face, and no doubt just as untidy. Perhaps even rakish by now. But at heart he was good and that thoughtless self-will of his was frequently a characteristic of the artistic temperament. One had to forgive artists much.

Reluctantly, Matthew Wade opened his eyes. He had come to the end of his memories, to the point where he would merely turn and go back to the beginning again. Too much introspection was a bad thing, so it was time to switch memory off.

Across the ward, he saw the familiar row of beds with their regular quota of visitors. He knew them all by sight. Chinese or Western. Wives, sons, daughters; parents, cousins, friends. He wondered if the pretty young wife, who visited bed number three, had arrived yet, but his view was blocked by a tall figure. It was silhouetted against the light of a window, so the face was invisible, but for some reason Matthew's attention was held. It couldn't be one of the doctors, because they never came near the wards during visiting hours.

But the set of those shoulders, the way he held his head . . . somehow he felt he had seen them before. He closed his eyes, then opened them again to find that the man had moved to his side and was standing very still, looking down on him.

He was oddly frightened. When memory conjured up faces from the past so vividly that one believed them to be actually present, there was cause for fear. He lay still, looking up at a bearded face which he had never seen before, yet somehow he knew.

'Matthew,' said the bearded man gently. 'Don't you know me?'

The old man's hands trembled on the bedcover and the man stooped and covered them with his own. Dear God, thought Clive, I never imagined these hands could grow so thin! The veins showed blue against the white and wrinkled skin, but they were still the hands which had once painted so brilliantly that the youthful Clive had been fascinated and awed by them.

He forced a light note into his voice, but the effort was great. He had not been so emotionally moved for years. 'It's me—Clive. The Prodigal Son. Remember?'

Tears streaked the old man's cheeks. He took a deep, quavering breath and growled, 'You're a bit late, aren't you?'

'Pretty late, Matt. Long overdue, in fact, but back in your life to stay.'

Their hands gripped. Clive was shocked again by the pathetic weakness of the master's. He had to force his glance away from them, and it was then that he saw the plaster cast about the man's ribs.

'What have you been doing now?' he quipped. 'Casting yourself in plaster? Since when have you gone in for modelling and sculpture, sir?'

It was the 'sir' that did it; the unconscious lapse into boyhood respect. It placed them immediately on the old footing, and, imperceptibly, Elisha's head lifted. He was no longer destitute and weak; he was Matthew Wade, R.A., being visited by his protégé. That was a different situation altogether and enabled him to look at Clive as he had looked at him in the old days—belligerently and fondly. He growled again. 'Almost made a fool of myself just now, m'boy. Thought I was imagining things! Put it down to old age and senility.'

'You'll cheat both, sir.'

'Aye,' Matthew agreed. 'Don't be taken in by this damned thing they've trussed me up in. I'm as active as ever I was.'

'Of course you are.'

'Well—almost. Doctor Diana has faith that I will be, so I must prove her right, mustn't I? How did you find me, by the way? I left the old address years ago.'

'I thought you must have done. I wrote you once and had no reply.'

'Did you expect one? I was an even worse letter writer than yourself!'

Clive answered guiltily, 'I should have written again.'

'But characteristically didn't. And stop staring at this damned straitjacket—I'm not helpless. I get into bed and take a nap every afternoon otherwise I wouldn't be lying here. As soon as this damned thing comes off, I'll be back at work again. If it comes to that, I could be working now. I can walk, sit, and stand while wearing it, and a damned sight more comfortable than when lying down. If I only had my materials here, there are a few interesting faces in this hospital that I would like to paint—that little nurse over there, with her fascinating mixture of Eastern and

Western blood, and Dr. Diana too. You should see that red hair of hers—Titian would have loved to paint her.'

'I've seen it,' Clive said. 'I've known her for quite some time.'

'The devil you have! She didn't tell me.'

'How could she know that *you* knew *me?*'

'You're right there. By the way, how did you track me down?'

'Through these—' Clive indicated a bundle of sketches on the bed. 'Why you kept these rubbishy things, I don't know.'

Matthew Wade's face lit up. 'So she fixed it, bless her! I asked her to. I suppose she told you? I thought it would be better if a man went—' He broke off. It was all up now, of course. Pretence was futile if Clive had seen that wretched room and the even more wretched district, and one glance at his face revealed that he had.

'Look,' he said anxiously, 'don't be deceived by those lodgings of mine. They're only temporary. I've had a run of ill-health, but I still have plenty of work lined up—outstanding commissions . . .' His voice trailed off. What was the use of lying? Since Clive had seen that room, he had also seen the worn-out materials and miserable canvases which had been painted over time and time again, until the surfaces were like nothing so much as solid wood. All would tell their own story. He said rather sheepishly, 'I always was a rotten liar,

177

wasn't I?'

Clive smiled. 'If you are lying, I'm glad, because now I can ask for your help.'

'*You* need *my* help? You passed beyond that a long time ago.'

'You're wrong. I need a complete new start. I need to work with a master, someone better and more experienced than myself. Call it a refresher course. I'd like to stay in Hong Kong, if you'll join forces with me.'

It was a full minute before Matt could trust himself to speak. 'You know damn well I can't afford to. If you saw my room in Lei Street, you know why.'

'Finance doesn't enter into this. I've made enough for both of us to live on comfortably for quite a time. I've made my mark in the theatre, but it's not really my scene. In particular, I'm tired of the people in it.'

He thought of Gloria, who had obviously thrown him over to pursue Jonathan Kinsale. Was he putting this idea up to old Matt just to spite her? He didn't believe so. The whole idea of remaining in Hong Kong and working as an independent artist again, no longer enduring temperamental outbursts in the theatre nor dictatorship of theatrical managements, appealed to him as nothing had done for a long time. And what he said was true—he did need the influence of his master again, not only in his work but in his life.

Of course, Gloria wouldn't like it. No doubt

she thought she would pick up the threads of their love affair when they returned to London, and that he would be ready to let her. If so, she was in for the shock of her life.

'Think about it, Matt. Remember that once upon a time we lived on *your* earnings. Don't be too proud to live on mine.'

The old man muttered something about disliking charity, at which Clive exploded, 'What's charitable about making use of a man? That's what I'd be doing—making use of you. I do need a refresher course—I've been involved in scenic design for so long that I've almost forgotten how to tackle a small canvas, and as for portraiture—! I do need your help, Matt. Come and share a studio with me. Be my critic and my fellow worker. That's what I'm trying to get out of you. I'm not giving you anything.'

It worked, and having made an unselfish gesture for the first time in his life, Clive felt a great deal more satisfied.

Matt held out his hand. 'It's a deal. Shake on it—'

As they did so, Clive saw Diana hovering by the ward door, and above the old man's head he nodded imperceptibly. She smiled and went away, but Staff Nurse Chang, coming to announce the close of visiting hours, was curious.

A voice beside her said casually, 'Well, Lotus Blossom, how are you these days?'

179

Dorothy had seen little of Chris Muldoon since the night he was ill; their only meeting had been when on duty and therefore brief. Once upon a time he would have lingered for a chat, or dropped into the ward kitchen for a cup of tea. In more serious moments, he had discussed his work and his ambitions, but since that night their relationship had cooled.

She had taken him at his word and kept out of his way, but her awareness of him had steadily increased. She put a brisk note into her voice to hide it.

'I'm very well, thank you, Mr. Muldoon. I wasn't expecting the house surgeon to visit the wards at this hour.'

'I'm making my round early. I go off duty at six and there are a couple of post-operational cases in this ward that I want to check on.'

'Beds Six and Twelve, behind the screens at the far end, facing each other.' Dorothy led the way, her neat little back erect, her step businesslike, her manner impersonal. He wished she would thaw. He missed their old friendliness. He knew the rift was his fault, but she gave him no chance to apologise. That stirred his male anger. *So why the hell should I try to?*

Walking down the ward beside her, he saw a visitor leaving Elisha's bed, and was surprised. 'I thought that man had no friends,' he commented.

'So did I. This is the first visitor he has ever

had. And it's funny—' Dorothy Chang broke off thoughtfully.

'What's funny?'

'Well, for one thing, the man asked for him by our nickname. Only the hospital staff knows him as Elisha. And for another—' She broke off. How could she say that it had struck her as odd that Doctor Diana should be lingering at the ward door, looking in Elisha's direction, and then smiling as she turned away, as if she had received a signal of some sort?

'For another?' he prompted.

Dorothy shrugged. 'Oh, nothing.'

She opened the screen around Bed Six, and once again assumed her professional manner. After that they were strictly formal until Chris left the ward.

On his way to Women's Medical, he met the Super.

'Feeling fit again, Muldoon?'

'Fine, thank you, sir.'

With a nod, Jonathan went on his way. As he turned the bend of the stairs leading down to the main hall, he paused. Two people were talking together down there, and from the look of things the conversation was very personal, for they were totally unaware of everything else.

Diana and Clive Field. So now he was visiting her at the hospital, was he? And very happy she was looking . . .

Jonathan went back upstairs. He wasn't

going to watch any tender leavetaking a second time.

Five minutes later, Diana was summoned over the intercom. 'Doctor Freeman, please report to the Superintendent's office immediately. Doctor Freeman, please!'

She was still looking happy when she entered the room, which only incensed him more.

'You want me, sir?'

Want you? he thought. If you only knew how much!

'I must point out, Doctor, that neither the medical staff nor the nursing staff are permitted personal visits at the hospital during duty hours. In future, kindly arrange private rendezvous away from the Kinsale.'

She was shocked into anger, but controlled it. She answered stonily, 'What private rendezvous are you referring to, sir?'

'Field's visit, of course. I presume you were saying goodbye to him down there in the hall.'

Her chin tilted.

'For the time being, yes. Is that all you wish to say to me, sir?'

She was as cool as a cucumber, which incensed him even further.

'That is all,' he answered curtly. 'For the present.'

Diana walked out of the room, hating him. How could she ever have imagined that such a man was human?

CHAPTER TWELVE

The knock knock on Gloria's dressing room door came between the second and third acts of *The Merchant of Venice.*

It was Clive.

'You're late,' she remarked coldly.

'For what? I wasn't aware of any appointment. Am I expected to make one? Is that the latest gimmick?'

She dismissed her dresser and went on studying her reflection in the mirror, thoughtfully retouching her make-up. She really did make a very good Portia indeed, and looked very striking in her Venetian lawyer's robes . . .

'I have news for you,' Clive said. 'I'm quitting the company at the end of the Festival and remaining in Hong Kong.'

'Well, how nice, darling! I'll be doing the same thing, so we can go on seeing each other. But alas, not so intimately as before.'

He stared. '*You*—staying in Hong Kong? You mean for that holiday you hinted at? If I know you, and I know you very well, you'll be bored in no time without the limelight and attendant publicity.'

'And what makes you think I won't get it?' she purred. 'As the wife of a well-known surgeon here, I shall be prominent in Hong

Kong society.'

'Good God, don't tell me you've got him to propose? Congratulations. I know you've been making a dead set at him, but this is quick going, even for you. But I thought you were anti-marriage—at least, you were whenever I suggested it.'

'Because I didn't want to become engaged to *two* men, darling.'

'Two! You don't mean—'

'—that I was engaged already? What else could I mean?'

He was struck dumb. It had always been Clive's boast that nothing could ever surprise him, but *this*!

'Do you mean you were already engaged to Kinsale when you began your affair with me?'

Gloria nodded. 'All firmly tied up long ago, and I have my sapphire and diamonds to prove it.'

'But you never told me that was an *engagement* ring. These days, when people wear rings on every finger, the third finger of the left hand no longer has any significance. You should have told me!'

'Why should I? Jonathan's work had brought him back to Hong Kong and mine kept me in London. I could hardly be expected to live the life of a nun in his absence. But now fate has brought us together again. It's really very romantic. If you're remaining here you really must come and visit us occasionally. Old friends will always be welcome. How long do you propose to stay?'

'Permanently,' he said curtly.

'But the company? You can't leave it in the lurch. You have a contract.'

'So have you, and I daresay you will break it as ably as I will. There is always a way out.'

'The management won't be pleased.'

'I know that. I'll be taken for a helluva lot of compensation and I'll pay it gladly. I'm going back to the work I really want to do, with a partner I really want to join up with.'

Her eyebrows arched. 'A female partner, I take it?'

'Wrong. A man.

'He's well on in his seventies and was the greatest friend and benefactor I ever had. Now I want to reciprocate, and in the process I'll be a damn' sight happier than I've been for years. I'll phone London in the morning and break the news, and the management can do their worst. They're entitled to and I won't put up a fight. I don't suppose I'll see anything of you for the rest of this run. I'll be coming to the theatre daily, of course, but I've a lot to fix up, the chief thing being an apartment which will also give us a good studio. I'm looking at one out at Repulse Bay tomorrow—beautiful spot, wonderful light. So wish me luck.'

Gloria blew him a kiss. 'Of course I do, darling. We both seem to be landing on our feet, don't we?'

185

But when the door closed behind him, she banged her fists on the dressing table, furiously. She didn't like being ditched by a man, even one she no longer wanted.

*   *   *

Although he no longer practised medicine, the hospital remained the greatest interest in Hammond Kinsale's life, along with his son. He was chairman of the hospital board of management, knew every member of the medical, nursing, and ward staffs, and took a fatherly interest in everyone, from the highest to the lowest.

Nor did he only attend the hospital for board meetings, he was a familiar figure in the long corridors, helping patients to master their crutches, wheeling the infirm, even writing letters and choosing library books for those unable to do these things for themselves. Voluntary work of this sort was no comedown to his way of thinking; it kept him in touch with medicine and kept at bay the boredom of retirement. He still felt that he belonged, which was the important thing.

So it was no surprise to Jonathan when his father thrust his white head round his office door. He was always glad to see him; often talked over cases with him, and valued his attentive silences when he needed a good listener. He needed one now, yet could not bring himself to reveal why. He was reluctant to admit the reason even to himself.

To come across his son sitting at his desk, his thoughts miles away and the papers before him obviously forgotten, was certainly a surprise to Hammond. He might upbraid him now and then for overdoing things, but Jonathan's devotion to the hospital and his passionate interest in his work were a source of pride to him. The only thing lacking in his son's life was the right woman, but he had made up his mind never to refer to that subject again.

So he surprised himself as much as Jonathan when he said without preamble, 'Are you and Gloria getting together again? I hope not. Of course, never having met her except briefly the other night, I may be in no position to judge, but it will make no difference if you believe that. I noticed her monopolising you at the theatre party, and I must say you appeared to be more than willing, because she went on monopolising you for the rest of the evening. She's beautiful, I admit, but not right for you.'

He knew he had said too much, that it would have been wiser to say nothing at all, but it was out now. He plunged on, 'I suppose I daren't ask what you were talking about? You can tell me to mind my own business, of course, but it appeared to be very personal, very intimate—important, perhaps?'

Jonathan roused. He had been sitting there

thinking about Diana ever since she stalked out of the room; thinking about Gloria, too, and the mess he had made of his life; thinking about Clive Field and wondering why men like that had women eating out of their hands. Apparently it made no difference to Diana that Clive had hurt her so much that she had been compelled to run to the other side of the world to get away from him. She was still enamoured, still ready to yield to him even though he had been involved with her flatmate as well, and even though his name was linked with Gloria's.

But mere involvement wasn't what he himself wanted with Diana. He wanted to tell her of his love, to ask her to marry him, but until she was willing to listen, he hung back. One false step could ruin a relationship before it was even established, and she was too precious to lose in such a way—unlike Gloria, whose departure for England was something he passionately desired despite all her blandishments. He knew full well that she would never settle down as the wife of a surgeon in the Far East, nor did he want her to. As far as he was concerned, there weren't any remnaits of their love affair to pick up, greatly as she might protest to the contrary. Thank heaven they had never married, or those dreams of a home and children would have ended in tragedy. Now those dreams were back with him, but with Diana at the heart of them.

Jerking out of his reverie, he looked at his father's kindly face. It held all the concern it had held for him as a child, though he was trying to hide it.

'Yes, Father, my conversation with Gloria *was* important. I was trying to convince her, once and for all, that there could never be anything between us, but she disagreed.'

'*Why,* in heaven's name? What justification can she possibly have for latching on to you again so determinedly?' demanded Hammond.

'She claims that it was I, not she, who went back on promises, and she's justified in that.'

'Not if she refused to live in the place where your work was based. Gloria should have been prepared to live with you in Hong Kong.'

'She's prepared to now. She insists that because she didn't officially agree to end our engagement (she never returned my ring, and is still wearing it), then she's still my fiancée and I am under an obligation to marry her.'

'But she would never settle down here! I know Hong Kong is a glamorous place for people with money, but society in a colony like this can be very insular. After her life in London and the public acclaim she is accustomed to, she would soon feel restricted, frustrated.'

'I told her that,' Jonathan said wearily. 'It made no difference. She declared she would make a good wife, that she would work hard at

189

it. She was dramatizing herself even as she spoke, seeing herself as the elegant hostess and the wife of a successful surgeon.'

'And didn't she see herself in that capacity when you became engaged?'

'I don't know what she thought, except that London held better opportunities, which it does in many ways, of course. But now Hong Kong has got through to her and she's determined to stay.'

'But not with you. You won't agree to that, I hope.'

'Never. I don't love her. I love—'

Jonathan bit Diana's name back and his father pretended not to notice, but he left his son's office well pleased, and very thoughtful.

*   *   *

Clive's visits to the hospital became a daily ritual to which he looked forward increasingly as the days passed. Sometimes he met Diana, but never for more than a few minutes. In the hospital he saw a whole new side of her—an efficient doctor, self-confident, popular with the staff and loved by her patients. It would be nice to have her around again, he reflected. Nice to have her living near. And this time he would really get to know her.

He cornered her one day and asked her to view some apartments with him. 'I'd like a woman's opinion on them,' he said.

'Since it will be occupied only by men, you don't need one, but if it's company you're after, I'll come along. Flat-hunting alone is a depressing business, I know. I was thankful to tumble into that one with Pearl after seeing some of the so-called "flats' advertised in London.'

'About Pearl—' he began, but Diana cut him short.

'You don't have to excuse or explain anything to me. She's my friend and I'm genuinely fond of her, besides which she was instrumental in getting me this job, for which I'm more than grateful. That makes up for a purely feminine weakness which I or any other woman could be capable of—the weakness of wanting another woman's man, and since you were apparently giving her a run too, who can blame her?'

'Her heart wasn't broken.'

'I'm glad about that, otherwise I would never forgive you.'

'So your friendship with her is still O.K. ?'

Diana nodded. 'Of course. I've heard from her since she flew back. With luck she'll shortly have a stop-over here, and she's definitely coming home for her next leave.'

'And your friendship with me?'

'I'd like it to stay that way.'

'Just friendship? No more?'

She nodded, half smiling at his vanity. Even now he couldn't believe that he would never

191

get her back.

'You aren't in love with anyone else, are you?' he asked suspiciously.

'Do I ask *you* questions like that?' she countered.

'That means you are, or you wouldn't dodge it. Who is he? Have I met him?'

'I'll dodge that one too, because it's none of your business. Have I ever questioned you about Gloria?'

'No, but now I don't mind if you do. It's all off between us. I've told her what I plan to do and she told me what *she* has plans to do. Both plans take us in opposite directions.'

'And what are hers?' Diana asked automatically. Not that she was really interested. When the Festival ended, Gloria would go out of her life as well as Clive's, so she was unimportant.

Clive laughed. 'You'll be surprised. I was astonished. She'll be staying in Hong Kong with her husband.'

'Her husband! I didn't know she had one.'

'She hasn't, yet, but apparently they have been engaged for a long time, kept apart only by work, his being here and hers in London. Not that that curbed her amorous activities! I knew she had been around and that there were other men besides me in her life, but not that she had ever committed herself to any particular one. But that isn't the really surprising thing. The big surprise is the man

192

she is going to marry. Two people more completely opposite I cannot imagine. However, they're getting together again, so the bond or the need, or whatever it is that unites a man and a woman, must still be there. Not that I can see their marriage working. Gloria will soon be bored with Hong Kong and hankering after the theatre again. Honestly, Diana, can you imagine a woman like Gloria settling down as the wife of a surgeon in the Far East?'

Diana froze. Her lips moved, but no sound came. She stared back at Clive and he saw that her shocked face was white. Good grief, he thought, *he* is the man she's in love with!

He put out a hand to steady her, but she pulled away, shaking her head as if blinded by tears. Then she was gone, stumbling a little in her haste.

CHAPTER THIRTEEN

Gloria was surprised, but pleased, by Hammond Kinsale's invitation to lunch.

I have never had a chance to talk to you, let alone get to know you—my own son's wife-to-be, he wrote. *Could you spare the time to give an old man that pleasure?*

So Jonathan had told his father the news; he had come round to her way of thinking and accepted the fact that their engagement was still on. And his father's note put the seal of approval on it. She was elated, and sent her acceptance at once, arriving at his penthouse only ten minutes late. Such punctuality was a big concession from a star, which he must surely appreciate.

As a discreet servant poured pre-lunch drinks, she glanced appreciatively round the luxury apartment, then turned to her host with a dazzling smile.

'What a beautiful home you have! I had no opportunity to really see it when we all came along after the theatre that night, but now—'

'But now, what do you think of it?'

'Precisely what I have begun to realise during this visit, that people in Hong Kong live at a very high standard indeed. Penthouses like this would cost a fortune in London.'

'They do here.'

'But the difference is that few people in London can now afford them. High taxation, high rates, inflation—'

'We have taxation here, too.'

'But look what life has to offer in return!'

'Such as?'

She waved a hand. 'Well—all this!' She strolled out on to the roof garden with its magnificent views of the South China Seas and the dragon mountains of Kowloon. 'Shall I tell you what I see from my flat on the Chelsea embankment? Battersea Power Station.'

'But if you don't let your glance stray so far, you see the loveliness of the Embankment, the elegant terraced houses, the fascination of river boats and barges, the beautifully designed Victorian lamps perched on the Embankment walls. People like Thomas Carlyle put their seal of approval on the Embankment, and now you, Gloria Dickson, whose name as an actress could shine even more brightly than it shines now. That is why I admire you for giving it all up. Jonathan has told me the news, and I am delighted. Grateful, too. Nothing could prove your devotion to my son more than your willingness to stay here as his wife.'

Gloria sipped her drink, uncertain how to answer. That suggestion that she was going to fade into oblivion was even a little frightening. But she could always go to London to do a play or to record a T.V. series. There would be no need to hide her light completely . . . she could have the best of both worlds.

Throughout lunch she maintained a light and inconsequential chatter, after which they settled down for coffee on the roof garden. It was ablaze with plants and shrubs and with garden furniture which might have been chosen from the most costly display at the Ideal Home Exhibition. The whole place reeked of money, she reflected, and smiled even more charmingly at her future father-in-law, glad that Jonathan was his sole heir.

She had never suspected that he came from a family so well-heeled. He had aways let her think that he was nothing but a newly qualified surgeon with no more than a house surgeon's pay ahead of him, and years of struggle too.

Well, it was no use bemoaning the fact that she had been short-sighted. He might have had the sense to tell her the truth, but at least she had found it out now. And just in time. She had drifted from man to man since Jonathan had returned to Hong Kong, always searching for the right one—which meant one who was rich, devoted, and ready to put her interests and desires before his own. For all these reasons each, in turn, had failed to qualify.

She was now approaching the wrong end of her thirties; another ten years and she would be in the wrong end of her forties, sinking into character parts unless she could raise the money for essential cosmetic surgery—and *that* marked the start of an actress's battle with age, every ten years back on the table again, having the creases ironed out and the contours lifted, and the cost going up as rapidly as world inflation. Not for *me*, vowed Gloria. I'll take what the gods have miraculously provided and I'm not letting it go this time. Fate must have brought me here for this very purpose.

'. . . behind a façade,' Hammond Kinsale finished.

She had missed the first part of the

sentence, so turned to him with beguiling penitence. 'Forgive me, Dr. Kinsale—'

'Everyone calls me Hammond. I hope you will.'

'Of course, though I must get used to calling you Father.'

'Not yet, surely,' he queried blandly.

'Well, you will be my father-in-law.'

'Of course. Forgive me for forgetting it, but never having met you until you arrived in Hong Kong, the idea takes some getting used to.'

She smiled. 'You soon will.'

He agreed, adding that there was plenty of time. She nodded happily.

'A whole lifetime.' She let her head drop against the softly cushioned back of a garden lounger. She felt languorous and content, like a very well-fed cat. 'What were you saying about a façade?'

'Merely that one shouldn't be taken in by it. One should try to see what lies behind. You are on the stage, so you should appreciate that appearances are deceptive, that scenery and props and costumes and make-up are all designed to give only an illusion of reality. It wouldn't be play-acting otherwise, would it?'

'I don't quite follow.'

Hammond smiled. 'It's perfectly simple. Most of the occupants of this luxury block are government officials, or high-up in international commercial organisations, or banks like the Shanghai and Hong Kong, with apartments like these provided for them. Or else they are part of organisation's like Jardine's. Jardine's were the drug-smuggling people who put Hong Kong on the map, but are eminently respectable now with more godowns than any other trading enterprise here.'

'Godowns?'

'The local name for warehouses—tea, jade, ivory, silks, precious metals, amber, gold, silver, wines. The commodities they trade in are endless. Firms like Jardine's deal in the lot and more besides, which is why they are the ones to amass the wealth. Government officials live handsomely, too—fine homes, fine cars, and all provided, so they can put on a show of wealth which they actually don't possess. Families like mine are no different, and hospitals like the Kinsale, which rely on private financial support, cannot go on for ever.' He gave a shrug of resignation. 'It is sad, but there it is! We will go under, and the government-run hospitals will flourish—the Queen Elizabeth which serves Kowloon and the New Territories, the Queen Mary on Hong Kong side, because it is the teaching facility for the Medical School of Hong Kong University, and the psychiatric hospital out at Castle Peak.'

He sighed. 'Compared with hospitals like the Queen Elizabeth, which contains an entire emergency hospital within its walls, plus clinics and about two thousand beds, hospitals like the Kinsale and the Baptist Hospital and the Seventh Day Adventist Hospital are pretty small fry, but the latter two have the edge on us financially because they are backed by their religions funds. So you see, my dear, that my days in this place are numbered. A year? Two years? A matter of months, more likely, though Jonathan tries to hide things.'

'What things?' Gloria was sitting up now, alert and suspicious.

'Imminent bankruptcy, for one. A setback in his career for another. For me, it doesn't matter. I can find some small and cheap apartment somewhere. At my age, my needs are few. But Jonathan will be hard hit, and he won't find it easy to get another appointment. Not such a high-ranking one, at any rate. Perhaps one of the Government hospitals might take him in a lesser capacity, but I think pride will prevent him from considering that. I will miss him, of course.'

'You mean—that—that—'

'That he will have to find some hospital job or other wherever he has the luck to find it. Australia and New Zealand seem the obvious stepping stones from here, but British doctors and surgeons have been flocking there— except to the Australian outback, which just might give him a chance, and in some of the isolated parts of New Zealand's South Island, which isn't so romantic as people think. Miles and miles of bush, or endless, empty plains. And wet. All those mountains! And winds straight off the South Pole . . .'

'Don't be absurd! A man with Jonathan's experience and training and ability would be wasted in such places.'

'No medical man is wasted where there are human beings to need him, my dear.'

Gloria didn't even hear the note of gentle reproof. Aghast, she declared she didn't believe him. 'How could a hospital so long established as the Kinsale go under?'

'Very easily. It has always been a financial struggle to maintain the place, and the board has only managed to do so by cutting salaries to the minimum. Jonathan is grossly underpaid, and as a family we haven't a bean behind us. When I die, I won't leave a penny, but after all, does it matter? Money is becoming more valueless every day.'

He reached over and patted her hand, saying encouragingly, 'Don't be alarmed, my dear—he will land on his feet somewhere. I believe New Guinea and remote islands in the Pacific are always crying out for medical help. Of course, living conditions are bad, and so is the pay, but what is there to spend one's money on in such places? And with you beside him, he will be content, I know.'

'But *I* won't!' She slammed down her coffee cup so hard that it rattled in its saucer. 'Why should I be? Why should a woman—*any* woman, but especially one with my talent!—be content to cut herself off from civilization, pinching and scraping and hob-nobbing with the natives and being smitten with yellow fever and heaven knows what else?'

'Oh, I shouldn't worry about that,' Hammond Kinsale said easily. 'You'll have a husband to doctor you. As for hob-nobbing with the natives, I shouldn't think they will be your sole company. There are bound to be other women. Missionaries' wives, schoolmasters' wives, even a nurse or two, I shouldn't wonder.' He hadn't the slightest idea of what conditions were like in New Guinea but, once launched, his fervour carried him on. 'You can't think what a comfort it is to me, to know that my son will have a loyal wife beside him. After living in that very comfortable house in the grounds of the hospital, stark living and working conditions will be difficult for him to get used to. And after the life we live here in Hong Kong—as you yourself have remarked, very luxurious indeed—the comparison will be even worse—'

She interrupted furiously, 'Do you mean to tell me that all *this* is merely a façade, that you can't really afford this penthouse and that Jonathan is equally hard?'

'I'm afraid so.' He assumed a guilty expression, like a schoolboy who had overspent his allowance. 'But one has to keep

201

up appearances, doesn't one? Especially in a Crown Colony like Hong Kong, where everyone isn't merely trying to keep up with the Joneses, but to be one step ahead of them. Of course, when the crash comes the doors of Hong Kong society will be shut on us, but that's what life is like in narrow Colonial circles. So different from London! But once you and Jonathan are man and wife, you won't miss London or the theatre or any of it, I know.' He beamed on her. 'Bless you for coming back into his life, Gloria. Oh, do you really have to go so soon? *What* a pity—just when we were getting to know each other!'

*   *   *

An hour or so later, well pleased with himself, Hammond hurried over to the hospital, and arrived just as old Elisha was being helped down the front steps into a waiting car, Matron on one side of him, Diana on the other, and Clive Field ready to take the wheel.

They were off for a run to Sha Tin, Diana told him as he halted beside them. 'They are going to sketch some of the temples there.' She indicated a load of art equipment on the back seat, newly purchased. She was delighted by the change in Matthew Wade, whom she could no longer think of as Elisha. His enthusiasm for this afternoon's trip made a whole new man of him.

Hammond was delighted too. The old man looked better than he had ever seen him. As the car drove away, with Elisha sitting erect in his plaster cast and not caring a fig for it, and Clive carefully driving to avoid unnecessary jolts, Hammond said, 'You've wrought a change in that man which I would never have believed possible, Matron.'

The woman beamed. 'Not I. Doctor Diana.'

'Not I,' contradicted Diana. 'Clive Field.'

She was about to relate the whole story when Jonathan came striding down the hospital steps. She wanted to run away, but forced herself to at least appear calm and collected, though she was far from feeling it. Ever since Clive had blurted out the truth to her, she had avoided Jonathan, and she was well aware that he noticed it, and was angered by it. But she could be angry too. He had made love to her—worse, he had made her fall in love with him—and all the time he belonged to another woman. It made no difference that Gloria had been living and working in London and he in Hong Kong; she was the woman who had really mattered to him all along, so much so that she could reappear in his life and he was ready and willing to take her back.

But the pain of it all was stronger than anger. Diana had scarcely slept these last few nights. There were shadows beneath her eyes and her face was pale. She remembered too well and too often those passionate moments in Jonathan's arms, the feel of his mouth devouring her own, the strength of his body pressed against hers, his arms holding her with longing and desire. His passion had been genuine enough, strong and demanding, hungry and fierce. And wonderful. More wonderful than anything she had ever experienced, even with Clive.

Looking back on that infatuation, it seemed a very immature thing. *She* had been immature until an older man, a man capable of a strong and deep and abiding love (but not for her—for Gloria Dickson) had fired her blood and made her realise what love could really be like, a thing strongly physical but also spiritual, the sublimation of sex.

She knew what she had to do, and somehow she would do it. The sooner she got away from Hong Kong the better.

She heard Matron talking to Jonathan's father. She was telling him about the new lease of life opening up for Elisha. 'But we can't call him that any more—he is Matthew Wade, a Royal Academician, very famous at one time and going to be again, Mr. Field says. I must say I'm pleased with that young man. I really didn't suspect he had it in him, but then, one can never judge by appearances, can one?'

'So I've just been telling a lunch visitor,' Hammond chuckled, but when Matron looked at him enquiringly, he merely shook his head and left her guessing. 'By the way, Matron, I presume you have heard that the board has approved the plans for the new extension? A whole new Casualty wing, with Pre- and Ante-Natal clinics, with Pediatrics to follow. We owe much of the hospital's success to you, don't we, Jonathan?'

His son had joined them. Doctor Diana was slipping away, but Jonathan's detaining hand on her arm forced her to remain. 'We do indeed,' he agreed, 'but what I am particularly pleased about is that the great improvement in our financial position ensures better pay for nurses and medical staff. The Kinsale has come a long way and is going even further.'

Matron nodded proudly. 'The press will be full of it. I can see the headlines in the *Morning Post* and *Standard* already!'

But not yet, thought Hammond with secret satisfaction. He had already intimated to editorial ears that the news was not yet official and that a statement would be released when the time came—which he would make sure was after Gloria's departure.

Matron said, 'I was just telling your father the story about Elisha, which he hadn't heard.'

Jonathan nodded. 'The hospital is buzzing with it, and no wonder. Field told me it was all Diana's doing. You must get her to give you the details, Father. She has been too busy to give them to me, which is why I had to get them from another source.'

He was looking at Diana intently, urgently,

205

and she gave a cool little smile and went back indoors. She heard him hurrying after her. The main hall was mercifully deserted.

'Dr. Freeman—as superintendent of this hospital I order you to wait. I want to talk to you. I saw you helping the old man into that car, and came after you. You are *not* going to escape this time.'

He was actually smiling, jubilant, not caring a damn that Matron and his father had watched him chase after her.

'You've been avoiding me, and I won't put up with it. There are things I have to say to you, things I have to tell you. In particular, about a chapter in my life which, thank God, will soon be over. Please, Diana—don't turn away. Hear me out.'

The sound of footsteps echoed behind them—Matron and his father entering the hospital. He didn't care. He had been trying to waylay Diana ever since Field had put him in the picture about everything, making him realise what a pig-headed fool he had been, but now that Gloria had telephoned he was determined not to be a fool any more.

He could still hear Gloria's voice, furious but determined, screaming down the line: 'Why weren't you honest with me? Well—I've found you out and just in time! I wouldn't marry you now if you went down on your knees and begged me to! And I'm returning your ring this time—and for good. By the time you receive it, I'll be on my way back to London; I'm catching the next flight out, so this is goodbye once and for all. Everything is over between us!'

He was so overjoyed that he didn't even bother to ask in what way he had been dishonest, or what guilt she ascribed to him. It didn't matter. Nothing mattered but the fact that at last, he was finally and permanently free of her. Once having made up her mind on something which she believed to be to her own benefit, Gloria would never retract.

With determination, he seized Diana's arm. 'If you won't listen to me, I will have you paged over the intercom and ordered to my office again.'

'Your office will suit me well, sir. I have something to say to *you.*'

He swept her up the stairs. At the top, he looked back, still holding her. Matron and Hammond were watching; Matron surprised but indulgent, his father amused and hopeful.

'Don't go away without seeing me, Father— I have news. Gloria has been on the phone. I'll tell you why when I have dealt with something more important.' So saying, Jonathan swept Diana on towards his office, flung open the door, propelled her inside and said, *'Now listen to me—'*

'No! You listen to me! I want to be released from my contract.'

'Never. Or, at least, not until I say so.'

She tried to speak again, but his lips came down on hers, silencing her. She tried to resist, and failed. She was carried away on that tide of passion again, this time more potently, more perilously, until her senses were drowning and only the strength of his arms prevented her from swaying. But with a superhuman effort, she pulled away.

'I mean it!' Her voice shook, but she clung to her determination. '*I mean it.* I want to be released from my contract, I want to leave this hospital, I want to get away from Hong Kong!'

'Running away again?' he demanded. 'Running away from love? You can't do it. You've tried it before, when it wasn't the real thing, so how can you hope to escape when it is?' He took her in his arms again. 'You think I don't mean it? Let me show you.'

He picked her up and carried her to a deep armchair, and sank into it, cradling her, stroking her hair, kissing her and murmuring again and again, 'I love you, Diana . . . I love you, my darling, my dearest love . . . I want you now and for ever, and I shall have you. I shall marry you. I am free of Gloria for all time. I know Field told you about my engagement to her. He has put me in the picture about everything, right from the day you asked him to meet you at the tea house across the road. I saw you come out with him and kiss him good-bye, and I was torn apart by jealousy . . .'

Diana gave a little sob, and clung to him,

and his mouth sought hers again, and for a long time there was no more talking between them until at last, reluctantly, Jonathan put her aside.

'My love, my darling love, if I go on kissing you, even holding you, I shall lose all self-control.'

He placed her gently in the chair and went to sit a long way from her.

'We have to talk about certain things; I want to explain certain things, and the first concerns Gloria. I fell wildly in love with her when I was in London some time ago, a mad infatuation from which I broke free, but when she arrived in Hong Kong she wanted to pick up the threads just where we had left off. By that time I had met you, and fallen in love with you—after believing that I could never love again. But the more I resisted Gloria, the more determined she became to re-establish our engagement, even declaring that it had never been broken because she had never agreed that it should be. She hadn't a hope in heaven of becoming my wife; having met you, I could never marry anyone else, but *I* thought that *you* were still infatuated with Clive Field, which meant that I hadn't a hope in heaven of becoming your husband. Now he has put me in the picture about that relationship—it is all over, isn't it, my darling? You don't love him any more, do you?'

She shook her head. 'No more,' she said,

choking a little on the words. 'If love it ever really was . . .'

'We have neither of us truly loved before, and I thank God for that, because now we will discover the real thing together.'

She crossed to him swiftly. 'I can't sit so far away from you! I love you, Jonathan. *I love you.*'

'Enough to marry me?' he asked tenderly.

'More than enough!'

There was a tap on the door. Without releasing her, Jonathan called; 'Come in!' and his father's white head appeared. Hammond seemed not in the least surprised to find Diana in his son's arms.

'I hoped it would be you,' Jonathan said. 'I have news. Gloria is on her way back to London—and out of my life. What brought about her change in mind I haven't the faintest idea, but thank heaven for it. The other item of news is even more wonderful—Diana has promised to marry me, and the wedding must be soon because I have waited far too long to find a girl like her . . .'

'Splendid! Splendid!' His father came across, hands outstretched to Diana, and she went to meet him eagerly.

He gave her a fatherly kiss. 'I hope you stay in our family for a very long time indeed, my dear.'

'She is going to stay as long as we both shall live,' Jonathan declared.

'That is what I mean—a very long time indeed.'

'I could scarcely believe my ears when Gloria telephoned,' his son continued, slipping his arm about Diana again. 'I wonder what made her suddenly change her mind . . .'

'I cannot imagine,' his father murmured, hiding a smile as he closed the door behind him. Locked again in each other's arms, they neither saw nor heard him go.

Still smiling, the old man went on his benign way. Passing the door of the ward kitchen on Lotus, he halted and thrust his head inside. 'Any chance of a cuppa —?'

He broke off as a flutter of white and a rustle of starched skirts caught his eye and his ear. He closed the door again quickly, but not before he glimpsed the man in there—the man in whose arms he had startled little Nurse Chang. So she had made it up with Chris Muldoon—more than made up, from the look of things. Something told Hammond that there had been a passionate sincerity in that mutual embrace.

Few things went on in the Kinsale Hospital that he didn't know about, and the rift between the house surgeon and the staff nurse on Lotus was certainly not one of them.

Well, well, well—this seemed to be a day for lovers' meetings!

And playing the part of an elderly Cupid in his son's life had been worth all those disgraceful lies . . .

And now there was another romance in the air! He decided to loiter in the corridor and to intercept anyone who approached the ward kitchen. He would do it casually, of course, and on no obvious pretext. Those two young people should be given as much time as possible to kiss and make up. It was the least an elderly Cupid could do for them.

Altogether, Hammond reflected happily, he was becoming very good at the job.